IN THE
GARDEN
OF THE
NORTH
AMERICAN
MARTYRS

Also by Tobias Wolff

Ugly Rumours (1975)
The Barracks Thief (1984)
Back in the World (1985)
This Boy's Life (1989)
In Pharaoh's Army (1994)
The Night in Question (1997)
Old School (2003)
Our Story Begins: New and Selected Stories (2008)
That Room (2008)

IN THE
GARDEN
OF THE
NORTH
AMERICAN
MARTYRS

with a new preface from the author

TOBIAS WOLFF

ecco
An Imprint of HarperCollinsPublishers

HarperCollins books may be purchased for educational, business, or sales promotional use. For information please e-mail the Special Markets Department at SPsales@harpercollins.com.

A paperback edition of this book was published in 2004 by Ecco, an imprint of HarperCollins Publishers.

FIRST ECCO DELUXE PAPERBACK EDITION PUBLISHED 2015.

The Library of Congress has catalogued a previous edition as follows:

Wolf, Tobias, 1945– In the Garden of the North American Martyrs
    Contents: In the garden of the North American Martyrs—Smoking—
    Poaching—etc.)
    I. Title
    PS3573.055815   813'.54   81-880
    ISBN 0-88001-497-0 (pbk.)

ISBN 978-0-06-239384-5 (deluxe pbk.)

20 21 22   DIX/LSC   0 9 8 7 6 5 4 3

FOR CATHERINE

Contents

Preface

This collection of short stories is not my first book, though I list it that way in my author bio, and on the Previous Publications page of later books. My first was a novel set in Vietnam, begun and abandoned during my tour there in '67–'68, then taken up again when I got back and started college, making whatever time I could for it while caught up in a demanding course of study. I finished the novel just before getting my degree, and sent it off to an agent I'd met through a friend. He thought it was terrific, and hoped to have good news for me very soon.

I did not hear any news very soon, and then, over many months, at long intervals, just a few polite rejections. I gave up hope for the novel and started another. For the next couple of years I worked different jobs—reporter, waiter, security guard (for Pinkerton, mind you, nothing but the best)—and had just started teaching high school in San Francisco when the agent wrote to say that my novel had been picked up in England by Allen & Unwin, "J. R. R. Tolkien's publisher." I was astonished. I'd figured the agent had given up, like me. Tolkien. I hadn't read him but of course I knew about his books, and that millions of them had been sold. If Allen & Unwin could do that for tall tales about wizards and dwarfs and fairies, think what they could do for this *serious* novel of mine, on a subject of great consequence.

I received an advance so modest that pride forbids my disclosing it. Let me say that Tolkien's profits did not trickle down to me. At least I didn't have to pay *them* to publish it, though at that point I probably—no, certainly—would have, just to see the damned thing between covers.

Speaking of covers: the design they sent me was ugly, but I hesitated to complain. The editor seemed enthusiastic about it, and selling books was his business. To question his judgment might cost me his good will, and then what would become of my novel? Anyway, what did I know about cover art? I might be wrong— once on the book itself, it might look great, or at least okay. Vain hope. When the finished novel finally arrived, the jacket looked even worse than in the proofs they'd sent. But it wasn't the outside of the novel that disappointed me.

I remember the day well. I'd come home from school to find the padded envelope from England leaning against my door. I didn't open it right away. Instead I popped a beer and went outside and sat on a cement wall overlooking the bay, savoring the moment. Being an author. An author, gazing into the distance. I slit the envelope and let the book, my book, slide into my hand. Winced at the cover, but it did have my name on it. I opened the book and began to read, and I saw that it was not good.

This was an embarrassing discovery. When I'd first sent out the finished manuscript some two years earlier it had seemed to me a fine novel; otherwise I wouldn't have wanted it published at all. Now, in the finality of print, I could see only its faults. Self-conscious prose. Characters too obviously at the service of the book's "moral," such as it was. Effortful attempts at wit. A "plot" with gears and levers showing. I put it aside, thinking perhaps I was being too hard on it, nervous as I was at exposing my work to readers for the first time, and fearful of criticism. But in looking at it again and again over the next few weeks I could only confirm my first judgment, and that remains true to this day.

There's no reason now to put the boot into what was an honest effort to write good fiction, however unsuccessful. And the truth is, my book did me a good turn. It allowed me to see that I was repeating the same mistakes with my second novel, and gave me the push I needed to try something else. For the last year or so I had been reading mostly short stories. They were never taught in my university course at Oxford—only English poetry and novels—and I felt a great sense of excitement in rereading not only the Hemingway and Fitzgerald stories I'd loved in years past, but in discovering Chekhov and Maupassant, Frank O'Connor and Isak Dinesen, Katherine Ann Porter and Flannery O'Connor and John Cheever. To read the best of their stories was to feel you'd witnessed a sort of miracle—the calling to life of a particular world with its own atmosphere and understandings, its people caught midstride in their progress from some felt but undefined past toward a future not revealed but implied by what we have seen of their natures, all in a few pages.

For years I had been brooding over an incident that happened in the boarding school I'd attended, where a boy had been expelled for an offense committed by another boy. It couldn't carry a novel, but I decided to try it as a story, highly fictionalized. I liked what came of the effort, and still liked it after I revised it, and liked it even more when I revised it again. I sent it off, and to my genuine surprise it was taken by *The Atlantic*. It's called "Smokers," and you'll find it in this book.

I was caught by the challenge of the form—to hold the world in a grain of sand—and its pleasures, not least the pleasure of finishing a piece of work in weeks, or at least months, rather than years. I devoted myself to writing stories. By then my reading had deepened to include several contemporary masters, Grace Paley and Raymond Carver among them, and I wrote with the hope of some day belonging to this company, which I saw as a sort of aristocracy. Those years of apprenticeship were among the happiest of my life—writing for the pure love of it, as there could be no question of riches for the writer of stories, and having my work appear in magazines and journals, and finally this book, which I was able to read with pride rather than mortification.

Those were also the years when our first son, Michael, was born and began to walk, and one of my clearest memories is of him wobbling into my office, attracted by the sound of the typewriter, and with grubby hands exploring the desktop, which he could not see, until finally I lifted him into my lap and let him hit the keys until they were properly jammed and he lost interest. Then I would put him down, free the keys, and go back to work.

Tobias Wolff
March 8, 2015

Next Door

I wake up afraid. My wife is sitting on the edge of my bed, shaking me. "They're at it again," she says.

I go to the window. All their lights are on, upstairs and down, as if they have money to burn. He yells, she screams something back, the dog barks. There is a short silence, then the baby cries, poor thing.

"Better not stand there," says my wife. "They might see you."

I say, "I'm going to call the police," knowing she won't let me.

"Don't," she says.

She's afraid that they will poison our cat if we complain.

Next door the man is still yelling, but I can't make out what he's saying over the dog and the baby. The woman laughs, not really meaning it, "*Ha! Ha! Ha!*," and suddenly gives a sharp little cry. Everything goes quiet.

"He struck her," my wife says. "I felt it just the same as if he struck me."

Next door the baby gives a long wail and the dog starts up again. The man walks out into his driveway and slams the door.

"Be careful," my wife says. She gets back into her bed and pulls the covers up to her neck.

The man mumbles to himself and jerks at his fly. Finally he gets it open and walks over to our fence. It's a white picket fence, ornamental more than anything else. It couldn't keep anyone out. I put it in myself, and planted honeysuckle and bougainvillea all along it.

My wife says, "What's he doing?"

"Shh," I say.

He leans against the fence with one hand and with the other he goes to the bathroom on the flowers. He walks the length of the fence like that, not missing any of them. When he's through he gives Florida a shake, then zips up and heads back across the driveway. He almost slips on the gravel but he catches himself and curses and goes into the house, slamming the door again.

When I turn around my wife is leaning forward, watching me. She raises her eyebrows. "Not again," she says.

I nod.

"Number one or number two?"

"Number one."

"Thank God for small favors," she says, settling back. "Between him and the dog it's a wonder you can get anything to grow out there."

I read somewhere that human pee has a higher acid content than animal pee, but I don't mention that. I would rather talk about something else. It depresses me, thinking about the flowers. They are past their prime, but still. Next door the woman is shouting. "Listen to that," I say.

"I used to feel sorry for her," my wife says. "Not any more. Not after last month."

"Ditto," I say, trying to remember what happened last month to make my wife not feel sorry for the woman next door. I don't feel sorry for her either, but then I never have. She yells at the baby, and excuse me, but I'm not about to get all excited over someone who treats a child like that. She screams things like *"I thought I told you to stay in your bedroom!"* and here the baby can't even speak English yet.

As far as her looks, I guess you would have to say she's pretty. But it won't last. She doesn't have good bone structure. She has a soft look to her, like she has never eaten anything but donuts and milk shakes. Her skin is white. The baby takes after her, not that you would expect it to take after *him*, dark and hairy. Even with his shirt on you can tell that he has hair all over his back and on his shoulders, thick and springy like an Airedale's.

Now they're all going at once over there, plus they've got the hi-fi turned on full blast. One of those bands. "It's the baby I feel sorry for," I say.

My wife puts her hands over her ears. "I can't stand another minute of it," she says. She takes her hands away. "Maybe there's something on TV." She sits up. "See who's on Johnny."

I turn on the television. It used to be down in the den but I brought it up here a few years ago when my wife came down with an illness. I took care of her myself—made the meals and everything. I got to where I could change the sheets with her still in the bed. I always meant to take the television back down when my wife recovered from her illness, but I never got around to it. It sits between our beds on a little table I made. Johnny is saying something to Sammy Davis, Jr. Ed McMahon is bent over laughing. He is always so cheerful. If you were going to take a really long voyage you could do worse than bring Ed McMahon along.

"Sammy," says my wife. "Who else is on besides Sammy?"

I look at the TV guide. "A bunch of people I never heard of." I read off their names. My wife hasn't heard of them either. She wants to know what else is on. "'*El Dorado*,'" I read. "'Brisk adventure yarn about a group of citizens in search of the legendary city of gold.' It's got two-and-a-half stars beside it."

"Citizens of what?" my wife asks.

"It doesn't say."

Finally we watch the movie. A blind man comes into a small town. He says that he has been to El Dorado, and that he will lead an expedition there for a share of the proceeds. He can't see, but he will call out the landmarks one by one as they ride. At first people make fun of him, but eventually all the leading citizens get together and decide to give it a try. Right away they get attacked by Apaches and some of them want to turn back, but every time they get ready the blind man gives them another landmark, so they keep riding.

Next door the woman is going crazy. She is saying things to him that no person should ever say to another person. It makes my wife restless. She looks at me. "Can I come over?" she says. "Just for a visit?"

I pull down the blankets and she gets in. The bed is just fine for one, but with two of us it's a tight fit. We are lying on our sides with me in back. I don't mean for it to happen but before long old Florida begins to stiffen up on me. I put my arms around my wife. I move my hands up onto the Rockies, then on down across the Plains, heading South.

"Hey," she says. "No Geography. Not tonight."

"I'm sorry," I say.

"Can't I just visit?"

"Forget it. I said I was sorry."

The citizens are crossing a desert. They have just about run out of water, and their lips are cracked. Though the blind man has delivered a warning, someone drinks from a poisoned well and dies horribly. That night, around the campfire, the others begin to quarrel. Most of them want to go home. "This is no country for a white man," one says, "and if you ask me nobody has ever been here before." But the blind man describes a piece of gold so big and pure that it will burn your eyes out if you look directly at it. "I ought to know," he says. When he is finished the citizens are silent: one by one they move away and lie down on their bedrolls. They put their hands behind their heads and look up at the stars. A coyote howls.

Hearing the coyote, I remember why my wife doesn't feel sorry for the woman next door. It was a Monday evening, about a month ago, right after I got home from work. The man next door started to beat the dog, and I don't mean just smacking him once or twice. He was beating him, and he kept beating him until the dog couldn't even cry any more; you could hear the poor creature's voice breaking. It made us very upset, especially my wife, who is an animal lover from way back. Finally it stopped. Then, a few minutes later, I heard my wife say, "Oh!" and I went into the kitchen to find out what was wrong. She was standing by the window, which looks into the kitchen next door. The man had his wife backed up against the fridge. He had his knee between her legs and she had her knee between his legs and they were kissing, really hard, not just with their lips but rolling their faces back and forth one against the other. My wife could hardly speak for a couple of hours afterwards. Later she said that she would never waste her sympathy on that woman again.

It's quiet over there. My wife has gone to sleep and so has my arm, which is under her head. I slide it out and open and close my fingers, considering whether to wake her up. I like sleeping in my own bed, and there isn't enough room for the both of us. Finally I decide that it won't hurt anything to change places for one night.

I get up and fuss with the plants for a while, watering them and moving some to the window and some back. I trim the coleus, which is starting to get leggy, and put the cuttings in a glass of water on the sill. All the lights are off next door except the one in their bedroom window. I think about the the life they have, and how it goes on and on, until it seems like the life they were meant to live. Everybody is always saying how great it is that human beings are so adaptable, but I don't know. A friend of mine was in the Navy and he told me that in Amsterdam, Holland, they have a whole section of town where you can walk through and from the street you can see women sitting in rooms, waiting. If you want one of them you just go in and pay, and they close the drapes. This is nothing special to the people who live in Holland. In Istanbul, Turkey, my friend saw a man walking down the street with a grand piano on his back. Everyone just moved around him and kept going. It's awful, what we get used to.

I turn off the television and get into my wife's bed. A sweet, heavy smell rises off the sheets. At first it makes me dizzy but after that I like it. It reminds me of gardenias.

The reason I don't watch the rest of the movie is that I can already see how it will end. The citizens will kill each other off, probably about ten feet from the legendary city of gold, and the blind man will stumble in by himself, not knowing that he has made it back to El Dorado.

I could write a better movie than that. My movie would be about a group of explorers, men and women, who leave behind their homes and their jobs and their families—everything they have known. They cross the sea and are shipwrecked on the coast of a country which is not on their maps. One of them drowns. Another gets attacked by a wild animal, and eaten. But the others want to push on. They ford rivers and cross an enormous glacier by dog sled. It takes months. On the glacier they run out of food, and for a while there it looks like they might turn on each other, but they don't. Finally they solve their problem by eating the dogs. That's the sad part of the movie.

At the end we see the explorers sleeping in a meadow filled with white flowers. The blossoms are wet with dew and stick to their bodies, petals of columbine, clematis, blazing star, baby's breath, larkspur, iris, rue—covering them completely, turning them white so that you cannot tell one from another, man from woman, woman from man. The sun comes up. They stand and raise their arms, like white trees in a land where no one has ever been.

Hunters in the Snow

Tub had been waiting for an hour in the falling snow. He paced the sidewalk to keep warm and stuck his head out over the curb whenever he saw lights approaching. One driver stopped for him but before Tub could wave the man on he saw the rifle on Tub's back and hit the gas. The tires spun on the ice.

The fall of snow thickened. Tub stood below the overhang of a building. Across the road the clouds whitened just above the rooftops, and the street lights went out. He shifted the rifle strap to his other shoulder. The whiteness seeped up the sky.

A truck slid around the corner, horn blaring, rear end sashaying. Tub moved to the sidewalk and held up his hand. The truck jumped the curb and kept coming, half on the street and half on the sidewalk. It wasn't slowing down at all. Tub stood for a moment, still holding up his hand, then jumped back. His rifle slipped off his shoulder and clattered on the ice, a sandwich fell out of his pocket. He ran for the steps of the building. Another sandwich and a package of cookies tumbled onto the new snow. He made the steps and looked back.

The truck had stopped several feet beyond where Tub had been standing. He picked up his sandwiches and his cookies and slung the rifle and went up to the driver's window. The driver was bent against the steering wheel, slapping his knees and drumming his feet on the floorboards. He looked like a cartoon of a person laughing, except that his eyes watched the man on the seat beside him. "You ought to see yourself," the driver said. "He looks just like a beach ball with a hat on, doesn't he? Doesn't he, Frank?"

The man beside him smiled and looked off.

"You almost ran me down," Tub said. "You could've killed me."

"Come on, Tub," said the man beside the driver. "Be mellow. Kenny was just messing around." He opened the door and slid over to the middle of the seat.

Tub took the bolt out of his rifle and climbed in beside him. "I waited an hour," he said. "If you meant ten o'clock why didn't you say ten o'clock?"

"Tub, you haven't done anything but complain since we got here," said the man in the middle. "If you want to piss and moan all day you might as well go home and bitch at your kids. Take your pick." When Tub didn't say anything he turned to the driver. "Okay, Kenny, let's hit the road."

Some juvenile delinquents had heaved a brick through the windshield on the driver's side, so the cold and snow tunneled right into the cab. The heater didn't work. They covered themselves with a couple of blankets Kenny had brought along and pulled down the muffs on their caps. Tub tried to keep his hands warm by rubbing them under the blanket but Frank made him stop.

They left Spokane and drove deep into the country, running along black lines of fences. The snow let up, but still there was no edge to the land where it met the sky. Nothing moved in the chalky fields. The cold bleached their faces and made the stubble stand out on their cheeks and along their upper lips. They stopped twice for coffee before they got to the woods where Kenny wanted to hunt.

Tub was for trying someplace different; two years in a row they'd been up and down this land and hadn't seen a thing. Frank didn't care one way or the other, he just wanted to get out of the goddamned truck. "Feel that," Frank said, slamming the door. He spread his feet and closed his eyes and leaned his head way back and breathed deeply. "Tune in on that energy."

"Another thing," Kenny said. "This is open land. Most of the land around here is posted."

"I'm cold," Tub said.

Frank breathed out. "Stop bitching, Tub. Get centered."

"I wasn't bitching."

"Centered," Kenny said. "Next thing you'll be wearing a nightgown, Frank. Selling flowers out at the airport."

"Kenny," Frank said, "you talk too much."

"Okay," Kenny said. "I won't say a word. Like I won't say anything about a certain babysitter."

"What babysitter?" Tub asked.

"That's between us," Frank said, looking at Kenny. "That's confidential. You keep your mouth shut."

Kenny laughed.

"You're asking for it," Frank said.

"Asking for what?"

"You'll see."

"Hey," Tub said, "are we hunting or what?"

They started off across the field. Tub had trouble getting through the fences. Frank and Kenny could have helped him; they could have lifted up on the top wire and stepped on the bottom wire, but they didn't. They stood and watched him. There were a lot of fences and Tub was puffing when they reached the woods.

They hunted for over two hours and saw no deer, no tracks, no sign. Finally they stopped by the creek to eat. Kenny had several slices of pizza and a couple of candy bars: Frank had a sandwich, an apple, two carrots, and a square of chocolate; Tub ate one hard-boiled egg and a stick of celery.

"You ask me how I want to die today," Kenny said, "I'll tell you burn me at the stake." He turned to Tub. "You still on that diet?" He winked at Frank.

"What do you think? You think I like hard-boiled eggs?"

"All I can say is, it's the first diet I ever heard of where you gained weight from it."

"Who said I gained weight?"

"Oh, pardon me. I take it back. You're just wasting away before my very eyes. Isn't he, Frank?"

Frank had his fingers fanned out, tips against the bark of the stump where he'd laid his food. His knuckles were hairy. He wore a heavy wedding band and on his right pinky another gold ring with a flat face and an "F" in what looked like diamonds. He turned the ring this way and that. "Tub," he said, "you haven't seen your own balls in ten years."

Kenny doubled over laughing. He took off his hat and slapped his leg with it.

"What am I supposed to do?" Tub said. "It's my glands."

They left the woods and hunted along the creek. Frank and Kenny worked one bank and Tub worked the other, moving upstream. The snow was light but the drifts were deep and hard to move through. Wherever Tub looked the surface was smooth, undisturbed, and after a time he lost interest. He stopped looking for tracks and just tried to keep up with Frank and Kenny on the other side. A moment came when he realized he hadn't seen them in a long time. The breeze was moving from him to them; when it stilled he could sometimes hear Kenny laughing but that was all. He quickened his pace, breasting hard into the drifts, fighting away the snow with his knees and elbows. He heard his heart and felt the flush on his face but he never once stopped.

Tub caught up with Frank and Kenny at a bend of the creek. They were standing on a log that stretched from their bank to his. Ice had backed up behind the log. Frozen reeds stuck out, barely nodding when the air moved.

"See anything?" Frank asked.

Tub shook his head.

There wasn't much daylight left and they decided to head back toward the road. Frank and Kenny crossed the log and they started downstream, using the trail Tub had broken. Before they had gone very far Kenny stopped. "Look at that," he said, and pointed to some tracks going from the creek back into the woods. Tub's footprints crossed right over them. There on the bank, plain as day, were several mounds of deer sign. "What do you think that is, Tub?" Kenny kicked at it. "Walnuts on vanilla icing?"

"I guess I didn't notice."

Kenny looked at Frank.

"I was lost."

"You were lost. Big deal."

They followed the tracks into the woods. The deer had gone over a fence half buried in drifting snow. A no hunting sign was nailed to the top of one of the posts. Frank laughed and said the son of a bitch could read. Kenny wanted to go after him but Frank said no way, the people out here didn't mess around. He thought maybe the farmer who owned the land would let them use it if they asked. Kenny wasn't so sure. Anyway, he figured that by the time they walked to the truck and drove up the road and doubled back it would be almost dark.

"Relax," Frank said. "You can't hurry nature. If we're meant to get that deer, we'll get it. If we're not, we won't."

They started back toward the truck. This part of the woods was mainly pine. The snow was shaded and had a glaze on it. It held up Kenny and Frank but Tub kept falling through. As he kicked forward, the edge of the crust bruised his shins. Kenny and Frank pulled ahead of him, to where he couldn't even hear their voices any more. He sat down on a stump and wiped his face. He ate both the sandwiches and half the cookies, taking his own sweet time. It was dead quiet.

When Tub crossed the last fence into the road the truck started moving. Tub had to run for it and just managed to grab hold of the tailgate and hoist himself into the bed. He lay there, panting. Kenny looked out the rear window and grinned. Tub crawled into the lee of the cab to get out of the freezing wind. He pulled his earflaps low and pushed his chin into the collar of his coat. Someone rapped on the window but Tub would not turn around.

He and Frank waited outside while Kenny went into the farmhouse to ask permission. The house was old and paint was curling off the sides. The smoke streamed westward off the top of the chimney, fanning away into a thin gray plume. Above the ridge of the hills another ridge of blue clouds was rising.

"You've got a short memory," Tub said.

"What?" Frank said. He had been staring off.

"I used to stick up for you."

"Okay, so you used to stick up for me. What's eating you?"

"You shouldn't have just left me back there like that."

"You're grown-up, Tub. You can take care of yourself. Anyway, if you think you're the only person with problems I can tell you that you're not."

"Is something bothering you, Frank?"

Frank kicked at a branch poking out of the snow. "Never mind," he said.

"What did Kenny mean about the babysitter?"

"Kenny talks too much," Frank said. "You just mind your own business."

Kenny came out of the farmhouse and gave the thumbs-up and they began walking back toward the woods. As they passed the barn a large black hound with a grizzled snout ran out and barked at them. Every time he barked he slid backwards a bit, like a cannon recoiling. Kenny got down on all fours and snarled and barked back at him, and the dog slunk away into the barn, looking over his shoulder and peeing a little as he went.

"That's an old-timer," Frank said. "A real graybeard. Fifteen years if he's a day."

"Too old," Kenny said.

Past the barn they cut off through the fields. The land was unfenced and the crust was freezing up thick and they made good time. They kept to the edge of the field until they picked up the tracks again and followed them into the woods, farther and farther back toward the hills. The trees started to blur with the shadows and the wind rose and needled their faces with the crystals it swept off the glaze. Finally they lost the tracks.

Kenny swore and threw down his hat. "This is the worst day of hunting I ever had, bar none." He picked up his hat and brushed off the snow. "This will be the first season since I was fifteen I haven't got my deer."

"It isn't the deer," Frank said. "It's the hunting. There are all these forces out here and you just have to go with them."

"You go with them," Kenny said. "I came out here to get me a deer, not listen to a bunch of hippie bullshit. And if it hadn't been for dimples here I would have, too."

"That's enough," Frank said.

"And you—you're so busy thinking about that little jailbait of yours you wouldn't know a deer if you saw one."

"Drop dead," Frank said, and turned away.

Kenny and Tub followed him back across the fields. When they were coming up to the barn Kenny stopped and pointed. "I hate that post," he said. He raised his rifle and fired. It sounded like a dry branch cracking. The post splintered along its right side, up towards the top. "There," Kenny said. "It's dead."

"Knock it off," Frank said, walking ahead.

Kenny looked at Tub. He smiled. "I hate that tree," he said, and fired again. Tub hurried to catch up with Frank. He started to speak but just then the dog ran out of the barn and barked at them. "Easy, boy," Frank said.

"I hate that dog." Kenny was behind them.

"That's enough," Frank said. "You put that gun down."

Kenny fired. The bullet went in between the dog's eyes. He sank right down into the snow, his legs splayed out on each side, his yellow eyes open and staring. Except for the blood he looked like a small bearskin rug. The blood ran down the dog's muzzle into the snow.

They all looked at the dog lying there.

"What did he ever do to you?" Tub asked. "He was just barking."

Kenny turned to Tub. "I hate you."

Tub shot from the waist. Kenny jerked backward against the fence and buckled to his knees. He folded his hands across his stomach. "Look," he said. His hands were covered with blood. In the dusk his blood was more blue than red. It seemed to belong to the shadows. It didn't seem out of place. Kenny eased himself onto his back. He sighed several times, deeply. "You shot me," he said.

"I had to," Tub said. He knelt beside Kenny. "Oh God," he said. "Frank. Frank."

Frank hadn't moved since Kenny killed the dog.

"Frank!" Tub shouted.

"I was just kidding around," Kenny said. "It was a joke. Oh!" he said, and arched his back suddenly. "Oh!" he said again, and dug his heels into the snow and pushed himself along on his head for several feet. Then he stopped and lay there, rocking back and forth on his heels and head like a wrestler doing warm-up exercises.

Frank roused himself. "Kenny," he said. He bent down and put his gloved hand on Kenny's brow. "You shot him," he said to Tub.

"He made me," Tub said.

"No no no," Kenny said.

Tub was weeping from the eyes and nostrils. His whole face was wet. Frank closed his eyes, then looked down at Kenny again. "Where does it hurt?"

"Everywhere," Kenny said, "just everywhere."

"Oh God," Tub said.

"I mean where did it go in?" Frank said.

"Here." Kenny pointed at the wound in his stomach. It was welling slowly with blood.

"You're lucky," Frank said. "It's on the left side. It missed your appendix. If it had hit your appendix you'd really be in the soup." He turned and threw up onto the snow, holding his sides as if to keep warm.

"Are you all right?" Tub said.

"There's some aspirin in the truck," Kenny said.

"I'm all right," Frank said.

"We'd better call an ambulance," Tub said.

"Jesus," Frank said. "What are we going to say?"

"Exactly what happened," Tub said. "He was going to shoot me but I shot him first."

"No sir!" Kenny said. "I wasn't either!"

Frank patted Kenny on the arm. "Easy does it, partner." He stood. "Let's go."

Tub picked up Kenny's rifle as they walked down toward the farmhouse. "No sense leaving this around," he said. "Kenny might get ideas."

"I can tell you one thing," Frank said. "You've really done it this time. This definitely takes the cake."

They had to knock on the door twice before it was opened by a thin man with lank hair. The room behind him was filled with smoke. He squinted at them. "You get anything?" he asked.

"No," Frank said.

"I knew you wouldn't. That's what I told the other fellow."

"We've had an accident."

The man looked past Frank and Tub into the gloom. "Shoot your friend, did you?"

Frank nodded.

"I did," Tub said.

"I suppose you want to use the phone."

"If it's okay."

The man in the door looked behind him, then stepped back. Frank and Tub followed him into the house. There was a woman sitting by the stove in the middle of the room. The stove was smoking badly. She looked up and then down again at the child asleep in her lap. Her face was white and damp; strands of hair were pasted across her forehead. Tub warmed his hands over the stove while Frank went into the kitchen to call. The man who had let them in stood at the window, his hands in his pockets.

"My friend shot your dog," Tub said.

The man nodded without turning around. "I should have done it myself. I just couldn't."

"He loved that dog so much," the woman said. The child squirmed and she rocked it.

"You asked him to?" Tub said. "You asked him to shoot your dog?"

"He was old and sick. Couldn't chew his food any more. I would have done it myself but I don't have a gun."

"You couldn't have anyway," the woman said. "Never in a million years."

The man shrugged.

Frank came out of the kitchen. "We'll have to take him ourselves. The nearest hospital is fifty miles from here and all their ambulances are out anyway."

The woman knew a shortcut but the directions were complicated and Tub had to write them down. The man told them where they could find some boards to carry Kenny on. He didn't have a flashlight but he said he would leave the porch light on.

It was dark outside. The clouds were low and heavy-looking and the wind blew in shrill gusts. There was a screen loose on the house and it banged slowly and then quickly as the wind rose again. They could hear it all the way to the barn. Frank went for the boards while Tub looked for Kenny, who was not where they had left him. Tub found him farther up the drive, lying on his stomach. "You okay?" Tub said.

"It hurts."

"Frank says it missed your appendix."

"I already had my appendix out."

"All right," Frank said, coming up to them. "We'll have you in a nice warm bed before you can say Jack Robinson." He put the two boards on Kenny's right side.

"Just as long as I don't have one of those male nurses," Kenny said.

"Ha ha," Frank said. "That's the spirit. Get ready, set, *over you go*," and he rolled Kenny onto the boards. Kenny screamed and kicked his legs in the air. When he quieted down Frank and Tub lifted the boards and carried him down the drive. Tub had the back end, and with the snow blowing into his face he had trouble with his footing. Also he was tired and the man inside had forgotten to turn the porch light on. Just past the house Tub slipped and threw out his hands to catch himself. The boards fell and Kenny tumbled out and rolled to the bottom of the drive, yelling all the way. He came to rest against the right front wheel of the truck.

"You fat moron," Frank said. "You aren't good for diddly."

Tub grabbed Frank by the collar and backed him hard up against the fence. Frank tried to pull his hands away but Tub shook him and snapped his head back and forth and finally Frank gave up.

"What do you know about fat," Tub said. "What do you know about glands." As he spoke he kept shaking Frank. "What do you know about me."

"All right," Frank said.

"No more," Tub said.

"All right."

"No more talking to me like that. No more watching. No more laughing."

"Okay, Tub. I promise."

Tub let go of Frank and leaned his forehead against the fence. His arms hung straight at his sides.

"I'm sorry, Tub." Frank touched him on the shoulder. "I'll be down at the truck."

Tub stood by the fence for a while and then got the rifles off the porch. Frank had rolled Kenny back onto the boards and they lifted him into the bed of the truck. Frank spread the seat blankets over him. "Warm enough?" he asked.

Kenny nodded.

"Okay. Now how does reverse work on this thing?"

"All the way to the left and up." Kenny sat up as Frank started forward to the cab. "Frank!"

"What?"

"If it sticks don't force it."

The truck started right away. "One thing," Frank said, "you've got to hand it to the Japanese. A very ancient, very spiritual culture and they can still make a hell of a truck." He glanced over at Tub. "Look, I'm sorry. I didn't know you felt that way, honest to God I didn't. You should have said something."

"I did."

"When? Name one time."

"A couple of hours ago."

"I guess I wasn't paying attention."

"That's true, Frank," Tub said. "You don't pay attention very much."

"Tub," Frank said, "what happened back there, I should have been more sympathetic. I realize that. You were going through a lot. I just want you to know it wasn't your fault. He was asking for it."

"You think so?"

"Absolutely. It was him or you. I would have done the same thing in your shoes, no question."

The wind was blowing into their faces. The snow was a moving white wall in front of their lights; it swirled into the cab through the hole in the windshield and settled on them. Tub clapped his hands and shifted around to stay warm, but it didn't work.

"I'm going to have to stop," Frank said. "I can't feel my fingers."

Up ahead they saw some lights off the road. It was a tavern. Outside in the parking lot there were several jeeps and trucks. A couple of them had deer strapped across their hoods. Frank parked and they went back to Kenny. "How you doing, partner," Frank said.

"I'm cold."

"Well, don't feel like the Lone Ranger. It's worse inside, take my word for it. You should get that windshield fixed."

"Look," Tub said, "he threw the blankets off." They were lying in a heap against the tailgate.

"Now look, Kenny," Frank said, "it's no use whining about being cold if you're not going to try and keep warm. You've got to do your share." He spread the blankets over Kenny and tucked them in at the corners.

"They blew off."

"Hold on to them then."

"Why are we stopping, Frank?"

"Because if me and Tub don't get warmed up we're going to freeze solid and then where will you be?" He punched Kenny lightly in the arm. "So just hold your horses."

The bar was full of men in colored jackets, mostly orange. The waitress brought coffee. "Just what the doctor ordered," Frank said, cradling the steaming cup in his hand. His skin was bone white. "Tub, I've been thinking. What you said about me not paying attention, that's true."

"It's okay."

"No. I really had that coming. I guess I've just been a little too interested in old number one. I've had a lot on my mind. Not that that's any excuse."

"Forget it, Frank. I sort of lost my temper back there. I guess we're all a little on edge."

Frank shook his head. "It isn't just that."

"You want to talk about it?"

"Just between us, Tub?"

"Sure, Frank. Just between us."

"Tub, I think I'm going to be leaving Nancy."

"Oh, Frank. Oh, Frank." Tub sat back and shook his head.

Frank reached out and laid his hand on Tub's arm. "Tub, have you ever been really in love?"

"Well—"

"I mean *really* in love." He squeezed Tub's wrist. "With your whole being."

"I don't know. When you put it like that, I don't know."

"You haven't then. Nothing against you, but you'd know it if you had." Frank let go of Tub's arm. "This isn't just some bit of fluff I'm talking about."

"Who is she, Frank?"

Frank paused. He looked into his empty cup. "Roxanne Brewer."

"Cliff Brewer's kid? The babysitter?"

"You can't just put people into categories like that, Tub. That's why the whole system is wrong. And that's why this country is going to hell in a rowboat."

"But she can't be more than—" Tub shook his head.

"Fifteen. She'll be sixteen in May." Frank smiled. "May fourth, three twenty-seven p.m. Hell, Tub, a hundred years ago she'd have been an old maid by that age. Juliet was only thirteen."

"Juliet? Juliet Miller? Jesus, Frank, she doesn't even have breasts. She doesn't even wear a top to her bathing suit. She's still collecting frogs."

"Not Juliet Miller. The real Juliet. Tub, don't you see how you're dividing people up into categories? He's an executive, she's a secretary, he's a truck driver, she's fifteen years old. Tub, this so-called babysitter, this so-called fifteen-year-old has more in her little finger than most of us have in our entire bodies. I can tell you this little lady is something special."

Tub nodded. "I know the kids like her."

"She's opened up whole worlds to me that I never knew were there."

"What does Nancy think about all of this?"

"She doesn't know."

"You haven't told her?"

"Not yet. It's not so easy. She's been damned good to me all these years. Then there's the kids to consider." The brightness in Frank's eyes trembled and he wiped quickly at them with the back of his hand. "I guess you think I'm a complete bastard."

"No, Frank. I don't think that."

"Well, you *ought* to."

"Frank, when you've got a friend it means you've always got someone on your side, no matter what. That's the way I feel about it, anyway."

"You mean that, Tub?"

"Sure I do."

Frank smiled. "You don't know how good it feels to hear you say that."

Kenny had tried to get out of the truck but he hadn't made it. He was jackknifed over the tailgate, his head hanging above the bumper. They lifted him back into the bed and covered him again. He was sweating and his teeth chattered. "It hurts, Frank."

"It wouldn't hurt so much if you just stayed put. Now we're going to the hospital. Got that? Say it—I'm going to the hospital."

"I'm going to the hospital."

"Again."

"I'm going to the hospital."

"Now just keep saying that to yourself and before you know it we'll be there."

After they had gone a few miles Tub turned to Frank. "I just pulled a real boner," he said.

"What's that?"

"I left the directions on the table back there."

"That's okay. I remember them pretty well."

The snowfall lightened and the clouds began to roll back off the fields, but it was no warmer and after a time both Frank and Tub were bitten through and shaking. Frank almost didn't make it around a curve, and they decided to stop at the next road-house.

There was an automatic hand-dryer in the bathroom and they took turns standing in front of it, opening their jackets and shirts and letting the jet of hot air breathe across their faces and chests.

"You know," Tub said, "what you told me back there, I appreciate it. Trusting me."

Frank opened and closed his fingers in front of the nozzle. "The way I look at it, Tub, no man is an island. You've got to trust someone."

"Frank—"

Frank waited.

"When I said that about my glands, that wasn't true. The truth is I just shovel it in."

"Well, Tub—"

"Day and night, Frank. In the shower. On the freeway." He turned and let the air play over his back. "I've even got stuff in the paper towel machine at work."

"There's nothing wrong with your glands at all?" Frank had taken his boots and socks off. He held first his right, then his left foot up to the nozzle.

"No. There never was."

"Does Alice know?" The machine went off and Frank started lacing up his boots.

"Nobody knows. That's the worst of it, Frank. Not the being fat, I never got any big kick out of being thin, but the lying. Having to lead a double life like a spy or a hit man. This sounds strange but I feel sorry for those guys, I really do. I know what they go through. Always having to think about what you say and do. Always feeling like people are watching you, trying to catch you at something. Never able to just be yourself. Like when I make a big deal about only having an orange for breakfast and then scarf all the way to work. Oreos, Mars Bars, Twinkies. Sugar Babies. Snickers." Tub glanced at Frank and looked quickly away. "Pretty disgusting, isn't it?"

"Tub. Tub." Frank shook his head. "Come on." He took Tub's arm and led him into the restaurant half of the bar. "My friend is hungry," he told the waitress. "Bring four orders of pancakes, plenty of butter and syrup."

"Frank—"

"Sit down."

When the dishes came Frank carved out slabs of butter and just laid them on the pancakes. Then he emptied the bottle of syrup, moving it back and forth over the plates. He leaned forward on his elbows and rested his chin in one hand. "Go on, Tub."

Tub ate several mouthfuls, then started to wipe his lips. Frank took the napkin away from him. "No wiping," he said. Tub kept at it. The syrup covered his chin; it dripped to a point like a goatee. "Weigh in, Tub," Frank said, pushing another fork across the table. "Get down to business." Tub took the fork in his left hand and lowered his head and started really chowing down. "Clean your plate," Frank said when the pancakes were gone, and Tub lifted each of the four plates and licked it clean. He sat back, trying to catch his breath.

"Beautiful," Frank said. "Are you full?"

"I'm full," Tub said. "I've never been so full."

*   *   *

Kenny's blankets were bunched up against the tailgate again.

"They must have blown off," Tub said.

"They're not doing him any good," Frank said. "We might as well get some use out of them."

Kenny mumbled. Tub bent over him. "What? Speak up."

"I'm going to the hospital," Kenny said.

"Attaboy," Frank said.

The blankets helped. The wind still got their faces and Frank's hands but it was much better. The fresh snow on the road and the trees sparkled under the beam of the headlight. Squares of light from farmhouse windows fell onto the blue snow in the fields.

"Frank," Tub said after a time, "you know that farmer? He told Kenny to kill the dog."

"You're kidding!" Frank leaned forward, considering. "That Kenny. What a card." He laughed and so did Tub. Tub smiled out the back window. Kenny lay with his arms folded over his stomach, moving his lips at the stars. Right overhead was the Big Dipper, and behind, hanging between Kenny's toes in the direction of the hospital, was the North Star, Pole Star, Help to Sailors. As the truck twisted through the gentle hills the star went back and forth between Kenny's boots, staying always in his sight. "I'm going to the hospital," Kenny said. But he was wrong. They had taken a different turn a long way back.

An Episode in the
Life of Professor Brooke

Professor Brooke had no real quarrel with anyone in his department, but there was a Yeats scholar named Riley whom he could not bring himself to like. Riley was flashy, so flashy that even his bright red hair seemed an affectation, and it was said that he'd had affairs with some of his students. Brooke did not as a rule give credit to these rumors, but in Riley's case he was willing to make an exception. He had once seen a very pretty girl leaving Riley's office in tears. Students did at times cry over bad grades, but this girl's misery was something else: it looked more like a broken heart than a C–.

They belonged to the same parish, and Brooke, who liked to sit in the back of the church, often saw Riley at Mass with his wife and their four red-haired children. Seeing the children and their father together, like a row of burning candles, always made Brooke feel more kindly toward Riley. Then Riley would turn to his wife or look around, and the handlebars of his unnecessarily large moustache would come into view, and Brooke would dislike him again.

The Sunday after he'd seen the girl come out of Riley's office Brooke watched him go up and take communion, then return to his seat with downcast eyes and folded hands. Was he praying, or was he trying to remember whether he'd checked his collar for stains? Where did Riley find the time, considering his tireless production of superficial articles and books, for romancing girls who had not yet mastered the English sentence, who were still experimenting with hair styles and perfumes? Did Mrs. Riley know?

Brooke raised these questions with his wife after lunch, after their children had left the table. They often talked about other people's infidelities, not in a mean or superior way, but out of a sense of relief that after sixteen years they were still in love. Brooke's wife said that a crying girl didn't mean much—girls cried all the time. In her opinion Brooke should not make up his mind about Riley until he knew more. Brooke was touched by his wife's innocence and generosity, and pretended to agree.

In November the regional chapter of the Modern Language Association met in Bellingham. Professor Brooke had been invited to take part in a panel discussion on the afternoon of the second day, and though he did not enjoy literary carnivals he hoped that he might bring some sanity to the meeting. He knew the work of the other panel members and judged that there was a real and present danger of the discussion becoming a brawl.

Just before he left, Brooke had a call from Riley. Riley was scheduled to read a paper that night and his car was on the blink. Could he have a ride? "Of course," Brooke said, but after he hung up he complained to his wife. "Dammit," he said, "I was looking forward to being alone." It wasn't only the loss of privacy that made him cross; he and Riley had quarreled at a tenure committee meeting the week before and he feared that Riley, who had no tact or sense of occasion, would renew the argument. Brooke did not want to fight his way to Bellingham with a man who wore powder-blue suits.

But Riley was taciturn, preoccupied. As they were leaving Seattle he asked Brooke to pull into a filling station so that he could make a telephone call. Brooke watched him in the booth, frowning at the receiver and gesticulating like a man practicing a speech. When he got back in the car he wore a theatrically tormented expression and Brooke felt obliged to ask whether there was anything wrong.

"Yes," Riley said, "but you don't want to hear about it, believe me." He said that he was having difficulties with the editor of his latest book.

Brooke didn't quite believe him. He wondered if it had something to do with the girl. Perhaps Riley had gotten her pregnant and was trying to dissuade her from having an abortion. "Let me know," he said, "if there's anything I can do."

"That's nice of you," Riley said. "You know, you remind me of a guy I knew in high school who was voted Nicest in the Class. No kidding." He hooked his arm over the seat and smiled at Brooke in a special way he had, curling his handlebars up and showing a flash of teeth. It looked as if he had somewhere come upon the phrase "roguish smile" and developed this expression to match it, and it drove Brooke absolutely crazy. "Tell me," Riley said, "what's the worst thing you've ever done?"

"The worst thing I've ever done?"

Riley nodded, showing more teeth.

For some reason Brooke panicked: his hands got wet on the steering wheel, his knees trembled, and he couldn't think straight.

"Forget it," said Riley after a time, and gave a little laugh, and hardly spoke again for the rest of the trip.

Brooke finally calmed down, but the question persisted. What *was* the worst thing he had ever done? One night when he was thirteen, and home alone, and had just finished off all the maraschino cherries in the refrigerator and gotten bored with sighting in the neighbors on the scope of his father's hunting rifle, he called the parents of a girl who had died of leukemia and asked to speak to her. That same year he threw a cat off a bridge. Later, in high school, he unthinkingly used the word "nigger" in front of a black classmate who considered Brooke his friend, and claimed that he had seduced a girl who had merely let him kiss her.

When Brooke recalled these things he felt pain—a tightening at the neck that pulled his head down and made his shoulders hunch, and a tingling in his wrists. Still, he doubted that Riley would be very impressed. Riley clearly had him down for a goody-goody. And, in a way, he was; that is, he tried to be good. When you tried to be good you ran the risk of seeming a prig, but what was the alternative? Brooke did not want to know. Yet at times he wondered if he had been too easily tamed.

The panel discussion was not a success. One of the members, a young man named Abbot from Oregon State University, had recently published a book on Samuel Johnson which attempted to define him as a poet and thinker of the Enlightenment. The thesis was so wrongheaded that Brooke had assumed it to be insincere, but this was not the case. Abbot seemed to think that his ideas did him credit, and persistently dragged them into conversations where they had no place. After one very long tirade Brooke decided to set him right and did so, he thought successfully, with few words.

"Excellent points," said the chairwoman, a Dryden scholar from Reed College who wore sunglasses and blew smoke out of her mouth as she talked. Turning to Abbot she said, "Is your speech finished?"

Abbot looked at her sharply, then nodded.

"Good," the chairwoman said. "To quote Samuel Johnson, that paradigm figure of the Enlightenment, 'No one would have wished it longer.'"

Abbot was crushed. His face went stiff with misery, and he sat without speaking for the rest of the discussion. Brooke felt embarrassed by the chairwoman's treatment of Abbot, not only because

she was unkind but because her unkindness was so distinctly pro-
fessorial.

When the panel ended he chatted with a woman he'd known
in graduate school. They were joined by an athletic-looking fellow whom Brooke supposed to be one of her students until she
introduced him as her husband. The disparity in their ages made
Brooke fidgety and he soon drifted away.

The room where the discussion had been held was actually
half of a long hall, divided by a folding partition. A meeting of
some kind had just begun on the other side. All the voices were
male, and Brooke guessed that they belonged to a group of scoutmasters who were holding a convention in the hotel. He stood at
one end of the refreshment table and ate little sandwiches with
pennants sticking out of them onto which someone had typed
literary quotations about food and drink. He saw Abbot at the
other end, looking out over the room and smirking to himself.
Brooke hoped that he would not become the kind of academic
who believes that his ideas are not accepted because they are too
profound and original. He went over to Abbot and showed him
one of his pennants.

"What did you get?" he asked.

"Nothing," Abbot said. "I'm on a diet." He stared into his coffee, the surface of which had an iridescent sheen.

"Tell me," Brooke said, "what are you working on now?"

Abbot drew a deep breath, put the cup down, and walked past
Brooke and out of the room.

"Ouch," said the woman on the other side of the table.

Brooke turned to her. She was striking; not beautiful, really,
but very blonde and heavily made-up. "You saw that?"

"Yes. You tried, anyway." She reached below the table and
brought up a fresh platter of sandwiches. "Have one," she said.
"Salami and cheese."

"No thanks. Those quotations are hard to swallow."

She lowered the platter, her face as red as if she'd been slapped.

Brooke turned one of the pennants with his finger. "You did all these, didn't you?"

"Yes."

"I'm very sorry I said that. I was just being clever."

"It's all right."

"I'm going to keep my mouth shut," Brooke said. "Every time I open it I hurt someone's feelings."

"I didn't really understand what the panel was all about," she said, "but he was the one who kept interrupting all the time. I thought you were nice. I could tell, listening to you, that I would like you. But that woman. If anybody ever talked to me like that I would die. I would just die."

She leaned toward Brooke and spoke quietly, as though imparting confidences. Her lips were unusually full and, like the Wife of Bath, she had a gap between her front teeth. Brooke was going to tell her that in Chaucer's time a gap between your teeth meant that you were a very sensual person, but he decided not to. She might take it wrong.

On the other side of the partition the scoutmasters were saying the Pledge of Allegiance.

"Where did you get all the quotes?" Brooke asked.

"From Bartlett's. It was a dumb idea."

"No it wasn't. It was very thoughtful." Brooke meant to end the conversation there, but the woman asked him several questions and he thought that he should ask her some questions in return. Her name was Ruth. She was a nurse at Bellingham General and had lived in the town all her life. She was unmarried. The local waiters' union, to which the caterers belonged, had gone on strike and Ruth had been asked to help out at the conference by a college teacher who belonged to her literary society.

"Literary society," Brooke said. "I didn't know they had them any more."

"Oh yes," Ruth said. "It's the most important thing in my life."

At that moment another woman ran up with a list of items for

Ruth to collect at the hotel kitchen. As Ruth turned away she looked over her shoulder and smiled.

By this time there were several people standing in line for sandwiches. Brooke moved to make room and soon found himself in a corner with a graduate student from his university who had just completed a dreary thesis on Ruskin. "Well," said the student, a tall boy with a stoop, "I guess the good doctor is turning over in his grave today."

"What good doctor?" Brooke asked, uncomfortable with this person who had spent four years of his life reading *The Stones of Venice*.

"Doctor Johnson."

"I don't know what you're talking about," Brooke said.

Riley, holding several sandwiches, joined them and the student had no chance to explain. "You really went after Abbot," Riley said.

"I didn't intend to go after anyone."

"You could have fooled me."

"It was a panel," Brooke said. "He spoke from his point of view and I spoke from mine. That's what we were supposed to do."

"You mean," Riley said, "that you spoke from the right point of view and he spoke from the wrong point of view."

"I think so. What do you think?"

"I don't know the period as well as I should," Riley said, "but I thought his ideas seemed original. They were interesting enough."

"Interesting," Brooke said, "in the way flat-Earth theories are interesting."

"I envy you," Riley said. "You're always so sure of yourself."

The student looked at his watch. "Uh-oh," he said. "I have to be going."

"I'm not always sure of myself," Brooke said. "But this time I am."

"I wasn't just thinking of the panel." Riley reminded Brooke of the tenure committee meeting the previous week. He wanted to know how Brooke could deny work to a woman with a sick husband and three children. He wanted to know how Brooke justified that to himself.

"We were asked to consider her professional qualifications," Brooke said. "She's a terrible teacher, as you very well know, and she hasn't published anything in over four years. Not even a book review."

"It was that simple, was it?"

"It wasn't simple at all," Brooke said. "If there was anything I could do for her short of giving her tenure I would do it. Now if you'll excuse me I'm going out for some fresh air."

A cold, salty breeze was blowing in off the water. The streets were empty. Brooke walked around the hotel several times, nodding to the doorman as he passed the entrance. The street lights were on, and some mineral embedded in the concrete made it glitter in a false and irritating way.

He decided that he was right and Riley wrong. But why did he feel so awful? It was ridiculous. He would have a bite to eat and drive home that very night. Riley could find another ride.

As he left the hotel restaurant Brooke saw the blonde woman—Ruth—standing in the lobby. He was about to turn away but just then she looked in his direction and smiled and waved. She was plainly glad to see him and Brooke decided to say hello. Not to do so, he thought, would be rude. They sat side by side in chairs that had, for some reason, been bolted to the floor. In the chairs across from them two scoutmasters were arm-wrestling. Ruth's perfume smelled like lavender; it came over Brooke in waves. He wanted to close his eyes and breathe it in.

"I called the library," she said, "but they didn't have either one of your books."

"That doesn't surprise me," Brooke said. He explained that they were too specialized to be of interest to the general public.

"I'd still like to read them," Ruth said. "There are people in the literary society who write things, haikus and so on, but I've never met anyone before who wrote a book, not to mention two books. Maybe," she said, "I can order them through a bookstore."

"That's possible," Brooke said, but he hoped she would not do that. His books were very difficult and she might think him pedantic.

"You know," she said, "I had a feeling I was going to see you tonight, either here or at the poetry reading."

"I didn't know there was one," Brooke said. "Who's the poet?"

"Francis X. Dillon. Is he a friend of yours?"

"No. Why do you ask?"

"Well, you're both writers."

"I've heard of him," Brooke said. "Of course." Dillon's poetry was very popular with Brooke's younger students and with his wife's mother. Brooke had picked up one of his books in a drugstore not long ago, intrigued by a blurb on the back claiming that the poet had been translated into twenty-three languages, including Hindu. As he turned the pages Brooke formed the image of a guru in a darkened cell reading these same dreadful verses by no other light than that of his own mystical aura. Now he thought it would be a shame to miss seeing Dillon in person.

The room was large and overheated and so crowded that the two of them had to stand in the back. The poet was half an hour late but not one person left, even though the air was stuffy and smelled bad.

Dillon arrived and without apology began to read. He was wearing a lumberjack shirt and a loose pair of khaki pants tied at the waist with a length of rope. All of the poems were about trees. They seemed to be saying that people had a lot to learn from trees. Trees were natural and uninhibited and didn't find it necessary to build roads and factories all over the place.

The principle by which the poems were arranged eluded Brooke until, during a pause, Dillon remarked that they would now be moving up into the aspen country. Then Brooke realized that the poems were grouped according to elevation. They had begun the ascent at sea level with the coastal redwoods and they'd been climbing steadily ever since. Brooke's attention wandered until finally the audience began to applaud; he joined in, assuming that they must have reached the timberline. Dillon read as an encore a very long piece which he described as "my other cedar poem," and left the room without a word to anyone when he was through.

"Isn't he wonderful!" Ruth said, as they stood applauding the empty podium.

Brooke gave a nod, the best he could manage.

She was not taken in. Later, at Lord George's, the bar where Ruth had suggested they go for a drink, she asked him why he didn't like the poems. He sensed that she was close to tears.

"I did like them," he said. "In fact, I loved them."

"Really?"

"Oh yes. I thought they were extraordinary."

"So did I," Ruth said, and began to describe her reactions to particular poems that Dillon had read. Brooke wondered why she had brought him to this place, with shields and maces and broadswords on the walls. She had said he would love it. What did that mean?

"Another thing I like about his poetry," Ruth said, "is you don't feel like killing yourself after you've read it."

"That's true," Brooke said. He noticed that two men at a nearby table were staring at her. They probably thought she was his wife. He could tell that they were wishing they were in his shoes.

"I went to a play last year," Ruth said, "a Shakespeare play, where this king gave everything away to his daughters—"

"*King Lear.*"

"That's the one. And then they turned on him and left him with nothing and gouged his best friend's eyeballs out and jumped on them. I don't understand why anybody, especially a really good writer like Shakespeare, would dream up junk like that."

"Life," Brooke said, "is not always uplifting."

"I know all about it," Ruth said, "believe me. But why should I rub my nose in it? I like to read about lovers. I like to read about how beautiful the mountains are, and the stars and so on. I like to read about people taking care of injured animals and setting them free again."

"You are very beautiful," Brooke said.

"You don't know what I look like," Ruth said. "This isn't my hair. It's a wig."

"I wasn't talking about what you look like," Brooke said, and this was partly true.

"Hello there," said Riley, who had come up to their table with Abbot. Both of them had their overcoats on, and Riley was doing his smile and blowing into his cupped hands. His face was white with a suggestion of blue, like milk. Brooke wondered why red-haired people went pale from the cold when others turned florid. It seemed strange. Abbot swayed back and forth in time to music only he could hear. "We've been making the rounds," Riley said. "Mind if we join you?"

Ruth moved closer to Brooke, and Riley slid into the booth and immediately began talking to her in a low voice. Abbot sat next to Brooke. He was quiet at first, then he abruptly leaned against Brooke and spoke into his ear as though it were a telephone receiver. "Been thinking about what you said today. Interesting. Very interesting. But all wrong." He began to repeat the arguments he had made earlier that day. When the waitress brought his drink, a tomato-juice concoction, he spilled most of it down the front of his shirt. "Can't be helped," he said, brushing away the handkerchief Ruth held out.

Brooke turned to Riley. "How did your paper go?"

"It was brilliant," Abbot said. "Brilliant beyond brilliant."

"Thank you," Riley said. "It did go quite well, I think."

"I'm sorry I missed it," Brooke said. "We went to the Dillon reading."

"I've just been hearing about it," Riley said. "Your friend . . ."

"Ruth," Brooke said.

"Ruth! What a beautiful name. 'Whither thou goest I will go; wherever thou lodgest,'" Riley said, looking right into her face, "'there also will I lodge.'"

This man is outrageous, Brooke thought, and groped under the table for Ruth's hand. He took it into his own and squeezed it. She squeezed back. What in the world am I doing? Brooke thought happily.

"Excuse me," Abbot said. He stood, then sat again heavily and pitched face down onto the table.

"I'd say it's taps for that soldier," Riley said.

"Would you mind taking him back to the hotel?" Brooke asked. "I'll see Ruth home."

Riley hesitated, and Brooke suspected that he was trying to think of a way to reverse the proposal. "All right," Riley said at last. "I'll call a cab."

At a table across the room a group of scoutmasters leaned together and sang:

> "Our paddles clean and bright
> Shining like sil-ver
> Swift as the wild goose flies
> Dip, dip and swing,
> Dip, dip and swing."

When the song was ended they howled in a way they all knew and one of them did a somersault on the floor.

Brooke had intended to go back to the hotel after he'd seen Ruth to her door, but he couldn't think of the right words to say and followed her inside. There were red pillows arranged in a circle around the living room, and a fat candle in the middle of the floor. Next to the door hung a framed, blown-up photograph of three sea gulls in flight with the sun behind them. Several wooden elephants, placed according to size like a growth chart, marched trunk-to-tail across the top of the bookshelf. "I believe in being honest," Ruth said.

"So do I," Brooke said, thinking that she was going to tell him about a boy friend or fiancé. He hoped so.

Ruth said nothing. Instead she brought both of her hands up to her hair and lifted it off like a hat. There was no hair underneath it, only a light down like a baby's. Ruth put the wig on a plaster bust that stood between a camel saddle and some foreign dolls on her bric-a-brac shelf. Then she faced Brooke. "Do you mind?" she asked.

"Of course not."

"Don't say 'Of course not.' It doesn't mean anything. Anyway, I've had a couple of bad experiences."

"No, Ruth. I don't mind." Brooke thought she looked exotic. She made him think of pictures he had seen of Frenchwomen whose heads had been shaved because they'd slept with Germans. He knew he should leave, but if he went now she would misunderstand and be hurt.

"I don't mind wearing the wig outside," Ruth said, "so that people won't get uncomfortable. But when I'm at home I'm going to be plain old me and that's that." She poured each of them a glass of wine and lit the candle. "I'm a floor person," she said, settling on a pillow. "If you want a chair there's one in the bedroom."

"That's all right," Brooke said. "I'm a floor person too." He tugged the knees of his trousers and sat Indian style across from her. As an afterthought he removed his suit jacket and folded it and laid it on the pillow next to him. "There," he said, and rubbed his hands together.

"I didn't think it would bother you," Ruth said. "I've noticed that creative people are usually interested in more than just looks."

"You look fine to me," Brooke said. "Exotic."

"You think so? Well, frankly, I'd rather have hair. I got pretty sick a few years ago and this is all I had left after the chemotherapy. They said it would grow back but it didn't. At least I'm still alive." She broke a string of wax off the candle and rolled it between her hands. "For a while there I wasn't doing too well."

"I'm sorry," Brooke said. "It must have been awful."

Ruth said that she had been just lying there, waiting for it to happen, when a friend of hers came for a visit and left a book of poems by Francis X. Dillon. "Do you know 'Sunrise near Monterey?'" she asked.

"Vaguely," Brooke said. He remembered that it ended with the command "Embrace!" He had thought it silly.

"That was the first poem I read," Ruth said. "When I got to the end I read it again and again and I just knew I was going to live. And here I am."

"You should write Dillon and tell him that."

"I did. I made up a poem and sent it to him."

"What did he say? Did he like it?"

"I don't know. I didn't want him to think that I was trying to get something out of him, so I didn't put down my address. Anyway, I started reading lots of poems and when I got out of the hospital I joined the Society." She named the poets who mattered to her— all of them, like Dillon, the sort who make Christmas albums, whose lines appear on the bottom of inspirational posters.

"What do you do there?" Brooke asked. "At the Society."

"We share."

"You lend each other books?"

"That," Ruth said, "and other things. Sometimes we read to each other and talk about life."

"It sounds like an encounter group."

"Isn't that why you write books?" Ruth asked. "To bring people together and help them live their lives?"

Brooke did not know exactly why he had written his books. He was not sure that his motives could stand that kind of scrutiny. "Let me hear your poem, Ruth. The one you sent Dillon."

"All right." She began to recite it from memory. Brooke nodded to the beat, which was forced and obvious. He barely heard the words. He was thinking that nothing he had ever thought or said could make a woman want to live again. "That was beautiful," he said when Ruth had finished the poem. "How about an encore?"

"That's the only poem I ever wrote except for one other, which is pretty personal." Ruth said that she couldn't write unless something made her do it, some really strong emotion.

"Then read something."

She slid a book from the shelf, opened it and cleared her throat. "'Sunrise near Monterey,'" she said, "by Francis X. Dillon." She glanced up at Brooke. "Oh," she said, "I love how you look at me."

"Read," Brooke said. He forced himself to smile and shake his head in the right places. After a time he began to enjoy it, and even allowed himself to believe what it was saying: that the world was beautiful and we were beautiful, and that we could be more beautiful if we just let ourselves go — if we shouted when we wanted to shout, ran naked when we wanted to run naked, embraced when we wanted to embrace.

Riley, wearing a green jacket with a plaid tie and plaid pants, came to Brooke's room the next morning. "You told me you wanted to get an early start," he said. "I hope this isn't too early for you."

Brooke felt Riley's gaze go over his shoulder to the bed. He had considered messing it up a little, but he couldn't bring himself to do it. Now he wished he had. "You should have called," he said.

Riley grinned. "I thought you might be up."

Heartsick, Brooke said very little on the drive home. Riley talked a blue streak and didn't seem to notice. He described the troubles he was having with the university press that was bringing out his new book, and gave Brooke a lot of advice on how to deal with editors. He made an anecdote out of his struggle to get

Abbot to his room the night before, and as they passed women on the road he rated their faces.

Riley's wife was standing at the picture window. She waved as Brooke pulled up to the house. Riley got his suitcase out of the back seat and stuck his head in the door just as Brooke was putting the car in gear. "Listen," he said. "I don't know what happened last night and I don't care. As far as I'm concerned I've never heard of anyone named Ruth."

"It wasn't like that," Brooke said.

"It never is," Riley said. He rapped the roof of the car with his knuckles and turned up the walk to his house.

Brooke decided not to tell his wife what he had done. In the past she had known everything about him, and it pleased him to be the man she thought him to be. Now he was different from what his wife thought, and if he were honest he would hurt her terribly. Brooke thought he had no right to do this. He would have to pretend that things were the same. He owed her that. It seemed hypocritical to him, but he could not think of a better way to settle the matter.

Without really being aware of it, Brooke saw the events of his life as forming chapters, and when he felt a chapter drawing to a close he liked to tie it up with an appropriate sentiment. Never again, he decided, would he sit in the back of the church and watch Riley. From now on he would sit in the front of the church and let Riley, knowing what he knew, watch him. He would kneel before Riley as we must all, he thought, kneel before one another.

Of course the chapter now ending for Professor Brooke was not ending for everyone else. Throughout that winter he found, in his mailbox at the university, anonymous love poems in envelopes with no return address.

And Brooke's wife, unpacking his clothes, smelled perfume on his necktie. Then she went through the laundry hamper and discovered the same heavy scent all over one of his shirts. There had to be an explanation, but no matter how long she sat on the edge of the bed and held her head in her hands and rocked back and forth she could not imagine what it might be. And her husband was so much himself that night, so merry and warm, that she felt unworthy of him. The doubt passed from her mind to her body; it became one of those flutters that stops you cold from time to time for a few years, and then goes away.

Smokers

I noticed Eugene before I actually met him. There was no way not to notice him. As our train was leaving New York, Eugene, moving from another coach into the one where I sat, managed to get himself jammed in the door between his two enormous suitcases. I watched as he struggled to free himself, fascinated by the hat he wore, a green Alpine hat with feathers stuck in the brim. I wondered if he hoped to reduce the absurdity of his situation by grinning as he did in every direction. Finally something gave and he shot into the coach. I hoped he would not take the seat next to me, but he did.

He started to talk almost the moment he sat down, and he didn't stop until we reached Wallingford. Was I going to Choate? What a coincidence—so was he. My first year? His too. Where was I from? Oregon? No shit? Way the hell and gone up in the boondocks, eh? He was from Indiana—Gary, Indiana. I knew the song, didn't I? I did, but he sang it for me anyway, all the way through, including the tricky ending. There were other boys in the coach, and they were staring at us, and I wished he would shut up.

Did I swim? Too bad, it was a good sport, I ought to go out for it. He had set a free-style record in the Midwestern conference the year before. What was my favorite subject? He liked math, he guessed, but he was pretty good at all of them. He offered me a cigarette, which I refused.

"I oughta quit myself," he said. "Be the death of me yet."

Eugene was a scholarship boy. One of his teachers told him that he was too smart to be going to a regular high school and gave him a list of prep schools. Eugene applied to all of them— "just for the hell of it"—and all of them accepted him. He finally decided on Choate because only Choate had offered him a travel allowance. His father was dead and his mother, a nurse, had three other kids to support, so Eugene didn't think it would be fair to ask her for anything. As the train came into Wallingford he asked me if I would be his roommate.

I didn't jump at the offer. For one thing, I did not like to look at Eugene. His head was too big for his lanky body, and his skin was oily. He put me in mind of a seal. Then there was the matter of his scholarship. I too was a scholarship boy, and I didn't want to finish myself off before I even got started by rooming with another, the way fat girls hung out together back home. I knew the world Eugene came from. I came from that world myself, and I wanted to leave it behind. To this end I had practiced over the summer an air of secret amusement which I considered to be aristocratic, an association encouraged by English movie actors. I had studied the photographs of the boys in the prep school bulletins, and now my hair looked like their hair and my clothes looked like their clothes.

I wanted to know boys whose fathers ran banks and held Cabinet office and wrote books. I wanted to be their friend and go home with them on vacation and someday marry one of their sisters, and Eugene Miller didn't have much of a place in those plans. I told him that I had a friend at Choate with whom I'd probably be rooming.

"That's okay," he said. "Maybe next year."

I assented vaguely, and Eugene returned to the problem he was having deciding whether to go out for baseball or lacrosse. He was better at baseball, but lacrosse was more fun. He figured maybe he owed it to the school to go out for baseball.

As things worked out, our room assignments were already drawn up. My roommate was a Chilean named Jaime who described himself as a Nazi. He had an enormous poster of Adolph Hitler tacked above his desk until a Jewish boy on our hall complained and the dean made him take it down. Jaime kept a copy of *Mein Kampf* beside his bed like a Gideons Bible and was fond of reading aloud from it in a German accent. He enjoyed practical jokes. Our room overlooked the entrance to the headmaster's house and Jaime always whistled at the headmaster's ancient secretary as she went home from work at night. On Alumni Day he sneaked into the kitchen and spiced up the visitors' mock turtle soup with a number of condoms, unrolled and obscenely knotted. The next day at chapel the headmaster stammered out a sermon about the incident, but he referred to it in terms so coy and oblique that nobody knew what he was talking about. Ultimately the matter was dropped without another word. Just before Christmas Jaime's mother was killed in a plane crash, and he left school and never returned. For the rest of the year I roomed alone.

Eugene drew as his roommate Talbot Nevin. Talbot's family had donated the Andrew Nevin Memorial Hockey Rink and the Andrew Nevin Memorial Library to the school, and endowed the Andrew Nevin Memorial Lecture Series. Talbot Nevin's father had driven his car to second place in the Monaco Grand Prix two years earlier, and celebrity magazines often featured a picture of him with someone like Jill St. John and a caption underneath quoting one of them as saying, "We're just good friends." I wanted to know Talbot Nevin.

So one day I visited their room. Eugene met me at the door and pumped my hand. "Well, what do you know," he said. "Tab, this here's a buddy of mine from Oregon. You don't get any farther up in the boondocks than that."

Talbot Nevin sat on the edge of his bed, threading snow-white laces through the eyes of a pair of dirty sneakers. He nodded without raising his head.

"Tab's father won some big race last year," Eugene went on, to my discomfort. I didn't want Talbot to know that I had heard anything about him. I wanted to come to him fresh, with no possibility of his suspecting that I liked him for anything but himself.

"He didn't win. He came in second." Talbot threw down the sneakers and looked up at me for the first time. He had china-blue eyes under lashes and brows so light you could hardly see them. His hair too was shock-white and lank on his forehead. His face had a molded look, like a doll's face, delicate and unhealthy.

"What kind of race?" I asked.

"Grand Prix," he said, taking off his shoes.

"That's a car race," Eugene said.

Not to have heard of the Grand Prix seemed to me evidence of too great ignorance. "I know. I've heard of it."

"The guys down the hall were talking about it and they said he won." Eugene winked at me as he spoke; he winked continuously as if everything he said was part of a ritual joke and he didn't want a tenderfoot like me to take it too seriously.

"Well, I say he came in second and I damn well ought to know." By now Talbot had changed to his tennis shoes. He stood. "Let's go have a weed."

Smoking at Choate was forbidden. "The use of tobacco in any form," said the student handbook, "carries with it the penalty of immediate expulsion." Up to this moment the rule against smoking had not been a problem for me because I did not smoke. Now it was a problem, because I did not want Eugene to have a bond with Talbot that I did not share. So I followed them downstairs to the music room, where the choir practiced. Behind the conductor's platform was a long, narrow closet where the robes were kept. We huddled in the far end of this closet and Talbot passed out cigarettes. The risk was great and the activity silly, and we started to giggle.

"Welcome to Marlboro Country," I said.

"It's what's up front that counts," Talbot answered. We were smoking Marlboros, not Winstons, and the joke was lame, but I guffawed anyway.

"Better keep it down," Eugene whispered. "Big John might hear us."

Big John was the senior dorm master. He wore three-piece suits and soft-soled shoes and had a way of popping up at awkward moments. He liked to grab boys by the neck, pinching the skin between his forefinger and thumb, squeezing until they cried. "Fuck Big John," I said.

Neither Talbot nor Eugene responded. I fretted in the silence as we finished our cigarettes. I had intended to make Eugene look timid. Had I made myself look frivolous instead?

I saw Talbot several times that week and he barely nodded to me. I had been rash, I decided. I had made a bad impression on him. But on Friday night he came up as we were leaving the dining hall and asked me if I wanted to play tennis the next morning. I doubt that I have ever felt such complete self-satisfaction as I felt that night.

Talbot missed our appointment, however, so I dropped by his room. He was still in bed, reading. "What's going on?" he asked, without looking up from his book.

I sat on Eugene's bed and tried not to sound as disappointed as I was. "I thought we might play a little tennis."

"Tennis?" He continued reading silently for a few moments. "I don't know. I don't feel so hot."

"No big deal. I thought you wanted to play. We could just knock a couple of balls around."

"Hell." He lowered the book onto his chest. "What time is it?"

"Nine o'clock."

"The courts'll be full by now."

"There's always a few empty ones behind the science building."

"They're asphalt, aren't they?"

"Cement." I shrugged. I didn't want to seem pushy. "Like I said, no big deal. We can play some other time." I stood and walked toward the door.

"Wait." Talbot yawned without covering his mouth. "What the hell."

As it happened, the courts were full. Talbot and I sat on the grass and I asked him questions I already knew the answers to, like where was he from and where had he gone to school the year before and who did he have for English. At this question he came to life. "English? Parker, the bald one. I got A's all through school and now Parker tells me I can't write. If he's such a goddamned William Shakespeare what's he teaching here for?"

We sat for a time without speaking. "I'm from Oregon," I said finally. "Near Portland." We didn't live close enough to the city to call it near, I suppose, but in those days I naively assumed everyone had heard of Portland.

"Oregon." He pondered this. "Do you hunt?"

"I've been a few times with my father."

"What kind of weapon do you use?"

"Marlin."

"30–30?"

I nodded.

"Good brush gun," he said. "Useless over a hundred yards. Have you ever killed anything?"

"Deer, you mean?"

"Deer, elk, whatever you hunt in Oregon."

"No."

Talbot had killed a lot of animals, and he named them for me: deer, moose, bear, elk, even an alligator. There were more, many more.

"Maybe you can come out West and go hunting with us sometime."

"Where, to Oregon?" Talbot looked away. "Maybe."

I had not expected to be humiliated on the court. My brother, who played tennis for Oregon State, had coached me through four summers. I had a good hot serve and my brother described my net game as "ruthless." Talbot ran me ragged. He played a kind of tennis different from any I had ever seen. He did not sweat, not the way I did anyway, or pant, or swear when he missed a shot, or get that thin quivering smile that tugged my lips whenever I aced my opponents. He seemed hardly to notice me, gave no sign that he was competing except that twice he called shots out that appeared to me to be well short of the line. I might have been mistaken, though. After he won the second set he walked abruptly off the court and went back to where we had left our sweaters. I followed him.

"Good game," I said.

He pulled impatiently at the sleeve of his sweater. "I can't play on these lousy asphalt courts."

Eugene made himself known around school. You did not wear belted jackets at Choate, or white buck shoes. Certainly you did not wear Alpine hats with feathers stuck in the brim. Eugene wore all three.

Anyone who didn't know who Eugene was found out by mid-November. *Life* magazine ran a series of interviews and pictures showing what it was like to be a student at a typical Eastern prep school. They had based their piece on research done at five schools, of which ours was one. Eugene had been interviewed and one of his remarks appeared in bold face beneath a photograph of students bent morosely over their books in evening study hall. The quotation: "One thing, nobody at Choate ever seems to smile. They think you're weird or something if you smile. You get dumped on all the time."

True enough. We were a joyless lot. Laughter was acceptable only in the sentimental parts of the movies we were shown on alternate Saturday nights. The one category in the yearbook to which everyone aspired was "Most Sarcastic." The arena for these trials of wit was the dining room, and Eugene's statements in *Life* did nothing to ease his load there.

However conspicuous Eugene may have been, he was not unpopular. I never heard anything worse about him than that he was "weird." He did well in his studies, and after the swimming team began to practice, the word went around that Eugene promised to put Choate in the running for the championship. So despite his hat and his eagerness and his determined grin, Eugene escaped the fate I had envisioned for him: the other students dumped on him but they didn't cast him out.

The night before school recessed for Christmas I went up to visit Talbot and found Eugene alone in the room, packing his bags. He made me sit down and poured out a glass of Hawaiian Punch which he laced with some murky substance from a prescription bottle. "Tab rustled up some codeine down at the infirmary," he explained. "This'll get the old Yule log burning."

The stuff tasted filthy but I took it, as I did all the other things that made the rounds at school and were supposed to get you off but never did, like aspirin and Coke, after-shave lotion, and Ben-Gay stuffed in the nostrils. "Where's Talbot?"

"I don't know. Maybe over at the library." He reached under his bed and pulled out a trunk-sized suitcase, made of cardboard but tricked up to look like leather, and began filling it with an assortment of pastel shirts with tab collars. Tab collars were another of Eugene's flings at sartorial trailblazing at school. They made me think of what my mother always told my sister when she complained at having to wear Mother's cast-off clothes: "You never know, you might start a fashion."

"Where are you going for Christmas?" Eugene asked.

"Baltimore."

"Baltimore? What's in Baltimore?"

"My aunt and uncle live there. How about you?"

"I'm heading on up to Boston."

This surprised me. I had assumed he would return to Indiana for the holidays. "Who do you know in Boston?"

"Nobody. Just Tab is all."

"Talbot? You're going to be staying with Talbot?"

"Yeah. And his family, of course."

"For the whole vacation?"

Eugene gave a sly grin and rolled his eyes from side to side and said in a confidential tone, almost a whisper: "Old Tab's got himself an extra key nobody knows about to his daddy's liquor closet. We aim to do some very big drinking. And I mean very big."

I went to the door. "If I don't see you in the morning, have a Merry Christmas."

"You bet, buddy. Same to you." Eugene grabbed my right hand in both of his. His fingers were soft and damp. "Take it easy on those Baltimore girls. Don't do anything I wouldn't do."

Jaime had been called home the week before by his mother's death. His bed was stripped, the mattress doubled over. All the pictures in the room had gone with him, and the yellow walls glared blankly. I turned out the lights and sat on my bed until the bell rang for dinner.

I had never met my aunt or uncle before. They picked me up at the station in Baltimore with their four children, three girls and a boy. I disliked all of them immediately. During the drive home my aunt asked me if my poor father had ever learned to cope with my mother's moods. One of the girls, Pammy, fell asleep on my lap and drooled on me.

They lived in Sherwood Park, a brick suburb several miles outside the city. My aunt and uncle went out almost every night and left me in charge of the children. This meant turning the television set on and turning it off when they had all passed out in front of it. Putting them to bed any earlier wasn't in the cards. They held on to everything—carpets, electrical cords, the legs of tables and chairs—and when that failed tried to injure themselves by scratching and gouging at their own faces.

One night I broke down. I cried for almost an hour and tried to call Talbot to ask him if I could come up to Boston and stay with him. The Nevins's number was unlisted, however, and after I washed my face and considered the idea again, I thought better of it.

When I returned to school my aunt and uncle wrote my father a letter which he sent on to me. They said that I was selfish and unenterprising. They had welcomed me as a son. They had opened their hearts to me, but I had taken no interest in them or in their children, my cousins, who worshipped the very ground I walked on. They cited an incident when I was in the kitchen reading and the wind blew all my aunt's laundry off the line and I hadn't so much as *asked* if I could help. I just sat there and went right on reading and eating peanuts. Finally, my uncle was missing a set of cuff links that had great sentimental value for him. All things considered, they didn't think my coming to Baltimore had worked out very well. They thought that on future vacations I would be happier somewhere else.

I wrote back to my father, denying all charges and making a few of my own.

After Christmas Talbot and I were often together. Both of us had gone out for basketball, and as neither of us was any good to the team—Talbot because of an ankle injury, me because I couldn't make the ball go through the basket—we sat together on the bench most of the time. He told me Eugene had spoiled his stepmother's Christmas by leaning back in an antique chair and breaking it. Thereafter I thought of Mrs. Nevin as a friend; but I had barely a month to enjoy the alliance because in late January Talbot told me that his father and stepmother had separated.

Eugene was taken up with swimming, and I saw him rarely. Talbot and I had most of our friends among the malcontents in the school: those, like Talbot, to whom every rule gave offense; those who missed their girl friends or their cars; and those, like me, who knew that something was wrong but didn't know what it was.

Because I was not rich my dissatisfaction could not assume a really combative form. I paddled around on the surface, dabbling in revolt by way of the stories I wrote for *off the record*, the school literary journal. My stories took place at "The Hoatch School" and concerned a student from the West whom I referred to simply as "the boy."

The boy's father came from a distinguished New York family. In his early twenties, he had traveled to Oregon to oversee his family's vast lumber holdings. His family turned on him when he married a beautiful young woman who happened to be part Indian. The Indian blood was noble, but the boy's father was disowned anyway.

The boy's parents prospered in spite of this and raised a large, gifted family. The boy was the most gifted of all, and his father sent him back East to Hoatch, the traditional family school. What he found there saddened him: among the students a preoccupation with money and social position, and among the masters hypocrisy and pettiness. The boy's only friends were a beautiful young dancer who worked as a waitress in a café near the school, and an old tramp. The dancer and tramp were referred to as "the girl" and "the tramp." The boy and girl were forever getting the tramp out of trouble for doing things like painting garbage cans beautiful colors.

I doubt that Talbot ever read my stories—he never mentioned them if he did—but somehow he got the idea I was a writer. One night he came to my room and dropped a notebook on my desk and asked me to read the essay inside. It was on the topic "Why Is Literature Worth Studying?" and it sprawled over four pages, concluding as follows:

> I think Literature is worth studying but only in a way. The people of our Country should know how intelligent the people of past history were. They should appreciate what gifts these people had to write such great works of Literature. This is why I think Literature is worth studying.

Talbot had received an F on the essay.

"Parker says he's going to put me in summer school if I flunk again this marking period," Talbot said, lighting a cigarette.

"I didn't know you flunked last time." I stared helplessly at the cigarette. "Maybe you shouldn't smoke. Big John might smell it."

"I saw Big John going into the library on my way over here." Talbot went to the mirror and examined his profile from the corner of his eye. "I thought maybe you could help me out."

"How?"

"Maybe give me a few ideas. You ought to see the topics he gives us. Like this one." He took some folded papers from his back pocket. "'Describe the most interesting person you know.'" He swore and threw the papers down.

I picked them up. "What's this? Your outline?"

"More like a rough draft, I guess you'd call it."

I read the essay. The writing was awful, but what really shocked me was the absolute lack of interest with which he described the most interesting person he had ever known. This person turned out to be his English teacher from the year before, whose chief virtue seemed to be that he gave a lot of reading periods and didn't expect his students to be William Shakespeare and write him a novel every week.

"I don't think Parker is going to like this very much," I said.

"Why? What's wrong with it?"

"He might get the idea you're trying to criticize him."

"That's his problem."

I folded up the essay and handed it back to Talbot with his notebook.

"You really think he'll give me an F on it?"

"He might."

Talbot crumpled the essay. "Hell."

"When is it due?"

"Tomorrow."

"*Tomorrow?*"

"I'd have come over before this but I've been busy."

We spent the next hour or so talking about other interesting people he had known. There weren't many of them, and the only one who really interested me was a maid named Tina who used to masturbate Talbot when she tucked him in at night and was later arrested for trying to burn the Nevins's house down. Talbot couldn't remember anything about her though, not even her last name. We finally abandoned what promise Tina held of suggesting an essay.

What eventually happened was that I got up at four-thirty next morning and invented a fictional interesting person for Talbot. This person's name was Miles and he was supposed to have been one of Talbot's uncles.

I gave the essay to Talbot outside the dining hall. He read it without expression. "I don't have any Uncle Miles," he said. "I don't have any uncles at all. Just aunts."

"Parker doesn't know that."

"But it was supposed to be about someone interesting." He was frowning at the essay. "I don't see what's so interesting about this guy."

"If you don't want to use it I will."

"That's okay. I'll use it."

I wrote three more essays for Talbot in the following weeks: "Who Is Worse—Macbeth or Lady Macbeth?"; "Is There a God?"; and "Describe a Fountain Pen to a Person Who Has Never Seen One." Mr. Parker read the last essay aloud to Talbot's class as an example of clear expository writing and put a note on the back of the essay saying how pleased he was to see Talbot getting down to work.

In late February the dean put a notice on the bulletin board: those students who wished to room together the following year had to submit their names to him by Friday. There was no time to waste. I went immediately to Talbot's dorm.

Eugene was alone in the room, stuffing dirty clothes into a canvas bag. He came toward me, winking and grinning and snorting. "Hey there, buddy, how they hangin'? Side-by-side for comfort or back-to-back for speed?"

We had sat across from each other at breakfast, lunch, and dinner every day now for three weeks, and each time we met he behaved as if we were brothers torn by Arabs from each other's arms and just now reunited after twenty years.

"Where's Talbot?" I asked.

"He had a phone call. Be back pretty soon."

"Aren't you supposed to be at swimming practice?"

"Not today." He smirked mysteriously.

"Why not?"

"I broke the conference butterfly record yesterday. Against Kent."

"That's great. Congratulations."

"And butterfly isn't even my best stroke. Hey, good thing you came over. I was just about to go see you."

"What about?"

"I was wondering who you were planning on rooming with next year."

"Oh, well, you know, I sort of promised this other guy."

Eugene nodded, still smiling. "Fair enough. I already had someone ask me. I just thought I'd check with you first. Since we didn't have a chance to room together this year." He stood and resumed stuffing the pile of clothes in his bag. "Is it three o'clock yet?"

"Quarter to."

"I guess I better get these duds over to the cleaners before they close. See you later, buddy."

Talbot came back to the room a few minutes afterwards. "Where's Eugene?"

"He was taking some clothes to the cleaners."

"Oh." Talbot drew a cigarette from the pack he kept hidden under the washstand and lit it. "Here," he said, passing it to me.

"Just a drag." I puffed at it and handed it back. I decided to come to the point. "Who are you rooming with next year?"

"Eugene."

"*Eugene?*"

"He has to check with somebody else first but he thinks it'll be all right." Talbot picked up his squash racket and hefted it. "How about you?"

"I don't know. I kind of like rooming alone."

"More privacy," said Talbot, swinging the racket in a broad backhand.

"That's right. More privacy."

"Maybe that South American guy will come back."

"I doubt it."

"You never know. His old man might get better."

"It's his mother. And she's dead."

"Oh." Talbot kept swinging the racket, forehand now.

"By the way, there's something I meant to tell you."

"What's that?"

"I'm not going to be able to help you with those essays any more."

He shrugged. "Okay."

"I've got enough work of my own to do. I can't do my work and yours too."

"I said okay. Parker can't flunk me now anyway. I've got a C+ average."

"I just thought I'd tell you."

"So you told me." Talbot finished the cigarette and stashed the butt in a tin soap dish. "We'd better go. We're gonna be late for basketball."

"I'm not going to basketball."

"Why not?"

"Because I don't feel like going to basketball, that's why not."

We left the building together and split up at the bottom of the steps without exchanging another word. I went down to the infirmary to get an excuse for not going to basketball. The doctor was out and I had to wait for an hour until he came back and gave me some pills and Kaopectate. When I got back to my room the dorm was in an uproar.

I heard the story from the boys in the room next to mine. Big John had caught Eugene smoking. He had come into Eugene's room and found him there alone and smelled cigarette smoke. Eugene had denied it but Big John tore the room apart and found cigarettes and butts all over the place. Eugene was over at the headmaster's house at this moment.

They told me the story in a mournful way, as though they were really broken up about it, but I could see how excited they were. It was always like that when someone got kicked out of school.

I went to my room and pulled a chair over to the window. Just before the bell rang for dinner a taxi came up the drive. Big John walked out of the dorm with two enormous cardboard suitcases and helped the driver put them in the trunk. He gave the driver some money and said something to him and the driver nodded and got back into the cab. Then the headmaster and the dean came out of the house with Eugene behind them. Eugene was wearing his hat. He shook hands with both of them and then with Big John. Suddenly he bent over and put his hands up to his face. The dean reached out and touched his arm. They stood like that for a long time, the four of them, Eugene's shoulders bucking and heaving. I couldn't watch it. I went to the mirror and combed my hair until I heard the door of the taxi bang shut. When I looked out the window again the cab was gone. The headmaster and the dean were standing in the shadows, but I could see Big John clearly. He was rocking back on his heels and talking, hands on his hips, and something he said made the headmaster laugh; not really a laugh, more like a giggle. The only thing I heard was the word "feathers." I figured they must be talking about Eugene's hat. Then the bell rang and the three of them went into the dining hall.

The next day I walked by the dean's office and almost went in and told him everything. The problem was, if I told the dean about Talbot he would find out about me, too. The rules didn't set forth different punishments according to the amount of smoke consumed. I even considered sending the dean an anonymous note, but I doubted if it would get much attention. They were big on doing the gentlemanly thing at Choate.

On Friday Talbot came up to me at basketball practice and asked if I wanted to room with him next year.

"I'll think about it," I told him.

"The names have to be in by dinner time tonight."

"I said I'll think about it."

That evening Talbot submitted our names to the dean. There hadn't really been that much to think about. For all I know, Eugene *had* been smoking when Big John came into the room. If you wanted to get technical about it, he was guilty as charged a hundred times over. It wasn't as if some great injustice had been done.

Face to Face

She met him at a fireworks display. That part of it was funny when she thought about it later.

Virginia had been set up. Not that anyone really *meant* to set her up—but it happened that way. The boy, for example. He'd stopped asking questions like "Where's Daddy?" "Why doesn't Daddy want to live with us any more?" Lately, he had taken to drawing pictures instead—immature pictures considering his age—with bug-bodied figures and fat suns with long yellow rays like spokes. All the pictures showed the same thing: a man and a woman with a little boy between them, holding hands and grinning off the page. "Ricky," she said, "why don't you draw something else?" He wouldn't, though. For this and for other reasons his teacher had begun to send Virginia strange notes.

Virginia's neighbors, Ben and Alice, played their part too. Alice kept telling her that it was a blessing in disguise that her husband had taken off. "You're free now, hon," said Alice. "You can find someone nice." Virginia had to admit that her husband wasn't any great shakes. But when he left, not saying a word, it took the life out of her, and she didn't think much about going out with men. Besides, she had her hands full with the boy.

Whenever Alice talked about her smart cousin from Everett, though, Virginia found herself listening. Alice always referred to him as "Poor Robert," and Virginia gathered that he had suffered some great wrong. In late June Alice told her that her cousin would be coming with them to see the fireworks display at Green Lake, and she invited Virginia and her son to join them. Virginia suspected that she had something in mind, but Alice had already told Ricky about the fireworks and he was all set to go; so she agreed.

Why not, she thought. She could probably do more for the boy if she stopped feeling so bad all the time.

From what Alice had told her about Robert, Virginia expected a distinguished, confident man, full of opinions and unlikely to be interested in her. Actually, he was shy. And polite. Whenever he reached for his cigarettes, he offered one to her even after she told him she didn't smoke. He was full of questions about her, though he had a way of looking off when he asked them. Robert's eyelids drooped and he had dense brown curls. A faint, acrid odor clung to him, like the smell of a newly painted room. He called Ricky "Crazylegs" and by the time they got to Green Lake he had promised to take the boy fishing—"As long as it's okay with your mom. Maybe she'd even like to come along," he added, looking out the window.

"We'll see," Virginia said.

Just after the fireworks started she went back to the parking lot with Robert to get some potato salad. They walked along without speaking, side by side. Finally, Virginia broke the silence.

"Alice says you went to college."

He nodded. "For a while, back in Michigan."

"What did you study?"

"Math, mostly. I was going to be an engineer. I didn't finish."

"That must be hard."

"It was a long time ago. Grin and bear it." He laughed.

"I mean the math must be hard."

"It wasn't that bad. I got all B's, except for some C's."

They got the potato salad from the car and started walking back. The only time they could really see was when a big flare or rocket went off. Robert took her arm gingerly when there were things they had to go around. Once they almost stepped on a couple lying under a blanket. Then a flare went off in descending stages with a big burst like an exclamation mark at the end, and they could see the couple moving together. Robert looked away quickly. Virginia thought that he did so because he didn't want to embarrass her by saying something about it. It did not occur to her until much later that he had looked away because he himself was embarrassed.

"So you live in Everett," she said.

"Just outside."

"What do you do there?"

Robert hesitated. "I'm a housepainter." He turned and looked her in the face for the first time. He was swallowed in shadows, and Virginia saw only his teeth clearly, moving up and down as he talked. "Maybe I could come over for a visit sometime."

"All the way from Everett? That would be a lot of trouble, wouldn't it?"

"I wouldn't mind," he said. "I really wouldn't."

When they got back Virginia sat down beside the boy. Ricky was lying on his back, watching the display—Alaska Candles, Starbursts, American Flags, each burst more dazzling than the one before. The boy's face changed colors with the rockets.

Robert called her often after that night. They usually went over to Alice and Ben's and drank and kidded around. When they didn't go there he took her and the boy out to the movies, once to a baseball game. He always behaved correctly: helped her with her coat, opened doors, and walked on the outside. When they parted, he would stare into her eyes and squeeze her hand with furtive, almost illicit intensity. More than a month passed before they went anywhere alone.

He took her to dinner at a place called Enrique's, where the waiters were all foreign and there was a violinist. Robert read the menu and told her about wines. "I like good food," he said. "It's my one weakness."

Virginia had guessed. Not that Robert was fat, exactly. More like stocky.

After dinner he took a big cigar from a metal tube and roasted the tip over the candle, all the while explaining how a really good cigar should be smoked. "You've got to respect it," he said, "almost like a person." Then he called the violinist over and had him play "Hungarian Tears" and a couple of other numbers. The violinist closed his eyes and smiled to himself as he played. Virginia squirmed and fiddled with her napkin. She was unable to meet the eyes of the people from the other tables who looked in their direction. She stared at Robert, who stared at the tip of his cigar. He gave the violinist a twenty dollar bill. "Twenty bucks isn't that much when you think about it. Look at all the training those guys have to go through."

Virginia nodded.

"Your husband—" Robert paused—waiting, Virginia thought, for her to supply a name. She said nothing. "How come the two of you split up?"

Virginia stared at him for a moment.

"We didn't split up. He left me."

These were hard words. It would have been easier to say, "Oh, we decided to take a vacation from each other." But when people said things like that to Virginia, she felt sorry for them, and she didn't want anyone feeling sorry for her. Nevertheless she felt ashamed.

"Left you?" Robert scowled at his cigar. "Why?"

"I don't know."

"Where—"

"I don't know where he went. It's been almost a year now."

"Maybe he didn't leave you. Maybe something happened to him."

"He left me."

"Tell me about him."

She began haltingly. Then, seeing that the stories about her husband fascinated Robert, she went on, telling more and more. Though he laughed in a way she didn't like, at least he laughed. So did she. Between stories, she said, "You've been married before, haven't you?"

He nodded. "How did you know?"

"Alice told me. What was she like?"

"Who? Florence? I don't know." Robert stood and fumbled for his wallet. "I'll get your coat. You want to go to the little girls' room or anything?"

They did not speak again, except politely, until he pulled up in front of her apartment building. He put his arm over the back of the seat. She tried to relax against it. He had left the engine running and the windshield wipers on.

Robert kissed her. He kissed her for a long time, and in the middle of it she opened her eyes and saw that his eyes were wide and startled. They held each other for a while. "I was wondering," Robert said softly.

"What?" She leaned back to look at him. "What were you wondering?"

"You think Crazylegs likes me?"

"Sure."

"Really?"

"Really."

"I'll bet sometimes he misses his dad."

"Sometimes. A lot of the time."

"A kid his age needs a father." Robert moved abruptly, banging his elbow against the steering wheel. "You ever been up to Vancouver?"

"To Vancouver? No."

"I was thinking maybe the two of us could go up there this weekend. Get to know each other."

He bent toward Virginia until they were face to face. She looked at him and wondered what he saw when he looked at her, if he saw his life running out. He had stopped breathing, or so it seemed, he was so quiet. The windshield wipers went back and forth. "All right," she said. "Sure. Why not?"

Their hotel was old and run down, but they had a big room with a fireplace. Virginia bounced on the bed and said how soft it was. She didn't mean anything by it, but Robert blushed. He adjusted the blinds. Then he took his clothes out of his suitcase and refolded them and put them in the bureau. He talked about how expensive the room was this time compared to three years ago when he had come up with the Everett Rifle Club.

At dinner Robert drank a lot of wine, and whatever it was that seemed to be troubling him passed off for a while. He told Virginia about a hiking trip he had gone on that the boy might like to take sometime. She reached out and touched his hand. "You're a good man," she said.

He frowned.

"Is there anything the matter?" she asked.

"I suppose you want to go upstairs," he said. He looked at Virginia.

"Not especially. Whatever you want."

"I thought I'd have a drink at the bar. You don't have to. You're probably tired."

"A little. A drink sounds nice, though." Virginia thought that he wanted a nightcap, to settle him after the long drive. When he ordered his fourth whisky, she understood that he planned to make a night of it. She had the feeling that he wanted either to get rid of her or drink her under the table. Probably he had something on his mind. "I think I'll run along to bed," she said finally.

"Go on. I'll be up in a minute."

Virginia went upstairs and bathed and waited for Robert in bed. She had a travel alarm clock with luminous hands. She watched the hour change twice before she heard Robert's key tumbling in the lock. He tiptoed over, carrying his shoes in his hand, and stood beside the bed, looking down at her. "Virginia?" he whispered.

She lay still. She did not reply, because she sensed he did not want her to.

Robert put his shoes under the bed and undressed quietly. He slipped between the sheets and curled up on the far side of the bed. Virginia wondered what she ought to do. Finally she decided to do nothing. He might get mad if he found out she was awake. Maybe he'd feel better in the morning. She wondered what she had done wrong.

Just after sunrise, Virginia started awake and felt Robert's hand on her breast. He was squeezing her softly. It surprised her and she looked over at him. He lay on his side, facing her, eyes closed. He moved his hand to her other breast. He squeezed there for awhile, then he threw his arm around her and pulled her close.

"Robert."

He didn't answer. Still with his eyes closed, he began to kiss her on her shoulders and neck. She hoped he wouldn't kiss her on the mouth. He rolled over on top of her and wedged his legs between hers. "Robert," she said again, but he seemed not to hear her. He forced her legs apart.

It didn't last long, and it hurt.

Robert rolled off and turned away. A few moments later he was sighing in sleep. At first Virginia wanted to kill him. After a while she decided she would settle for understanding him. She took a long bath. When she came out of the bathroom Robert was sitting on the edge of the bed, fully dressed, studying a map of Vancouver. He smiled at Virginia and stood up. "Good morning."

She dipped her head in his direction and waited. After what had happened she expected him to say something.

Instead he dropped the map and pointed toward the bathroom. "You all through in there?"

"Yes."

"You women." He shook his head. "I didn't know whether you were taking a bath or going for a swim."

"If you wanted to get in you should have knocked."

"Don't worry about it." He pecked her on the cheek as he went past her.

Robert didn't come out until after she was dressed. "Boy, you look nice," he said, rubbing his hands together.

Virginia could not look at him. "Just for you," she said.

They walked around Vancouver all morning. Robert read things to her from a tourist booklet. "It's better exercise than going on one of those busses," he explained, "and we won't have to put up with a bunch of people from God knows where." They ate lunch in a cafeteria he had noticed earlier in the day, and then they went to a movie. Virginia had never been to a movie in the daytime, not since she was a little kid anyway, and it made her uneasy. Most of the people in the theater were older men.

After he'd finished his popcorn Robert reached over and pressed Virginia's hand. Then he started to stroke the inside of her thigh.

"Please, Robert," she whispered. "Not here."

He pulled away from her. "What?"

Virginia had the idea that Robert was prepared to deny that he'd touched her. She shook her head. "Nothing," she said.

"Too bad old Crazylegs isn't with us." Robert took a sip of his Pepsi. "He'd get a kick out of this movie."

"Let's go, Robert."

"What's wrong?"

"I want to go." She stood and walked up the aisle. She waited for him in the lobby. Robert bought another popcorn on the way out and offered some to her. She shook her head. Outside they walked up the street in the direction of a logging museum.

At dinner that night Virginia asked Robert about his marriage. She had told him more about her husband on the drive up, and he had laughed about her husband's idea of style, the high life, his own possibilities. Virginia had discovered what it was she didn't like about Robert's laughter. It was superior. Her husband had been ridiculous, but not much more ridiculous than most people. Anyway, Robert had enjoyed a certain freedom with her past and she wanted something back.

But Robert kept talking about his old girlfriends instead. "I hope it doesn't bother you," he said. "It's ancient history." They'd been nuts about him, he said, but he'd had to cut them loose because it just didn't feel right. Most of them came from rich, classy backgrounds—daughters of colonels and district attorneys. "You can't sell yourself cheap," he told Virginia. "You've got to hold out for Miss Right. Or Mr. Right." He smiled. "As the case may be."

She said, "Tell me about your wife."

Robert turned his mouth down and stared into his glass. "Florence was a whore."

"What do you mean, Robert?"

"You know."

"No, I don't. Did she actually go out and sell herself to men? For money?"

Robert shrugged. "She was an amateur. She had to give it away." He almost smiled at his own joke. "I should have listened to my aunt," he went on. "She saw through Florence the first time they met."

"Then why did you marry her?" Virginia hoped that he would tell her that he had married out of love.

"Had to." He grinned. "You know how it is."

"Then you have a child!"

He shook his head. "Miscarriage."

"Where is Florence now?"

"I don't know. Still in Detroit, I guess. I don't know. I don't care."

"Is she alone?"

"No. She managed to get this guy to marry her. Don't ask me how."

"What guy?"

"The guy she was fooling around with."

"There was just one? One man?"

"One that I know of."

"But you called her a whore."

Robert's nostrils flared and his brows crept together. He panted softly. "You women," he said.

Virginia was afraid—not that Robert would hit her, but afraid.

"How come we started talking about Florence, anyway?" Robert said. "The hell with her." He stood. "Come on, let's go have a drink."

"I don't want any more to drink. You go ahead if you want."

He walked her to the lobby, and they waited for the elevator without speaking. He moved towards her a little, his eyes on her face, and she thought he wanted to kiss her. He looked unhappy. Maybe his wife had been a whore. Virginia wanted to believe that. She moved forward slightly, ready to receive his kiss, but he suddenly looked down and rummaged in his pocket.

"Here's the key," he said.

She could feel the color on her cheeks. She took the key.

"See you later," he said, and shuffled toward the bar, his arms dangling.

Virginia was sleeping when Robert came in. She only became aware of him when he slid on top of her. At first she didn't know where she was or what was happening. She sat up and pushed him away. She didn't remember screaming, but she might have, because Robert leaped out of bed and started looking around. "Jesus," he said, "what's wrong?"

"Oh, Robert." She rubbed her eyes, trying not to cry. "Please don't do that."

"Don't do what?"

"Oh, God." She covered her face.

Robert sat on the bed. "You don't like me, do you?"

"Sure I do. I'm here, aren't I?"

"I don't mean like that. I mean in bed."

She looked at him, hunched against the cold of the night. "No. Not that way. Not when I'm asleep."

He nodded grimly. "Whatever you say," he muttered.

Neither of them slept well. Virginia could feel Robert's misery. She softened. In the morning she reached out to him and began rubbing his back. She had to do this. She rubbed his back, his neck, his shoulders. When she touched his legs he tensed. Then he pushed her hands away and rolled over. "Okay," he said. He reached out for her.

"No, Robert. It's over. I want to go home."

They said little during the drive back, until they crested a hill and saw a lake far below. "Boy," Robert said, "that's really something."

"It sure is."

"When I used to see things like that," he went on, "I used to wish I had someone to see it with me." He looked at Virginia and laughed.

She saw that he was in some pain. She touched his hand. "I know what you mean. It's bad, sometimes, being alone."

"Not to complain," he said. "I do all right. It's different with men and women. The minute a woman gets alone she starts looking for someone."

"So do men."

Robert moved his hand away from Virginia's. "Some men," he said.

"It's natural, Robert, really. All of it. There's nothing to be ashamed of."

He looked at her with sudden panic and she knew that he was deciding at that moment always to be alone. She started out of herself, became enormous in her pity for him. "Don't give up, Robert. Not just because it didn't work with me." She wanted to say more but he had left her, gone back to his injury. She exercised her pity on him. The road slipped under the tires. Virginia stared greedily ahead.

Poor Robert, she thought.

Passengers

Glen left Depoe Bay a couple of hours before sunup to beat the traffic and found himself in a heavy fog; he had to lean forward and keep the windshield wipers going to see the road at all. Before long the constant effort and the lulling rhythm of the wipers made him drowsy, and he pulled into a gas station to throw some water in his face and buy coffee.

He was topping off the tank, listening to the invisible waves growl on the beach across the road, when a girl came out of the station and began to wash the windshield. She had streaked hair and wore knee-length, high-heeled boots over her blue jeans. Glen could not see her face clearly.

"Lousy morning for a drive," she said, leaning over the hood. Her blue jeans had studs poking through in different patterns and when she moved they blinked in the light of the sputtering yellow tubes overhead. She threw the squeegee into a bucket and asked Glen what kind of mileage he got.

He tried to remember what Martin had told him. "Around twenty-five per," he said.

She whistled and looked the car up and down as if she were thinking of buying it from him.

Glen held out Martin's credit card but the girl laughed and said she didn't work there.

"Actually," she said, "I was kind of wondering which way you were headed."

"North," Glen said. "Seattle."

"Hey," she said. "What a coincidence. I mean that's where I'm going, too."

Glen nodded but he didn't say anything. He had promised not to pick up any hitchhikers; Martin said it was dangerous and socially irresponsible, like feeding stray cats. Also Glen was a little browned off about the way the girl had come up to him all buddy-buddy, when really she just wanted something.

"Forget it," she said. "Drive alone if you want. It's your car, right?" She smiled and went back into the station office.

After Glen paid the attendant he thought things over. The girl was not dangerous—he could tell by how tight her jeans were that she wasn't carrying a gun. And if he had someone to talk to there wouldn't be any chance of dozing off.

The girl did not seem particularly surprised or particularly happy that Glen had changed his mind. "Okay," she said, "just a sec." She stowed her bags in the trunk, a guitar case and a laundry sack tied at the neck like a balloon, then cupped her hands around her mouth and yelled, "Sunshine! Sunshine!" A big hairy dog ran out of nowhere and jumped up on the girl, leaving spots of mud all over the front of her white shirt. She clouted him on the head until he got down and then pushed him into the car. "In back!" she said. He jumped onto the back seat and sat there with his tongue hanging out.

"I'm Bonnie," the girl said when they were on the road. She took a brush out of her purse and pulled it through her hair with a soft ripping noise.

Glen handed her one of his business cards. "I'm Glen," he said.

She held it close to her face and read it out loud. "Rayburn Marine Supply. Are you Rayburn?"

"No. Rayburn is my employer." Glen did not mention that Martin Rayburn was also his roommate and the owner of the car.

"Oh," she said, "I see, here's your name in the corner. Marine Supply," she repeated. "What are you, some kind of defense contractors?"

"No," Glen said. "We sell boating supplies."

"That's good to hear," Bonnie said. "I don't accept rides from defense contractors."

"Well, I'm not one," Glen said. "Mostly we deal in life jackets, caps, and deck furniture." He named the towns along the coast where he did business, and when he mentioned Eureka, Bonnie slapped her knee.

"All right!" she said. She said that California was her old stomping grounds. Bolinas and San Francisco.

When she said San Francisco Glen thought of a high-ceilinged room with sunlight coming in through stained glass windows, and a lot of naked people on the floor flopping all over each other like seals. "We don't go that far south," he said. "Mendocino is as far as we go." He cracked the window a couple of inches; the dog smelled like a sweater just out of mothballs.

"I'm really beat," Bonnie said. "I don't think I slept five straight minutes last night. This truck driver gave me a ride up from Port Orford and I think he must have been a foreigner. Roman fingers and Russian hands, ha ha." She yawned. "What the hell, at least he wasn't out napalming babies."

The fog kept rolling in across the road. Headlights from passing cars and trucks were yellow and flat as buttons until they were close; then the beams swept across them and lit up their faces. The dog hung his head over the back of the seat and sighed heavily. Then he put his paws up alongside his ears. The next time Glen looked over at him the dog was hanging by its belly, half in front and half in back. Glen told Bonnie that he liked dogs but considered it unsafe to have one in the front seat. He told her that he'd read a story in the paper where a dog jumped onto an accelerator and ran a whole family off a cliff.

She put her hand over the dog's muzzle and shoved hard. He tumbled into the back seat and began noisily to clean himself. "If everybody got killed," Bonnie said, "how did they find out what happened?"

"I forget," Glen said.

"Maybe the dog confessed," Bonnie said. "No kidding, I've seen worse evidence than that hold up in court. This girl friend of mine, the one I'm going to stay with in Seattle, she got a year's probation for soliciting and you know what for? For smiling at a guy in a grocery store. It's a hell of a life, Glen. What's that thing you're squeezing, anyway?"

"A tennis ball."

"What do you do that for?"

"Just a habit," Glen said, thinking that it would not be productive to discuss with Bonnie his performance at golf. Being left-handed, he had a tendency to pull his swing and Martin had suggested using the tennis ball to build up his right forearm.

"This is the first time I've ever seen anyone squeeze a tennis ball," Bonnie said. "It beats me how you ever picked up a habit like that."

The dog was still cleaning himself. It sounded awful. Glen switched on the tape deck and turned it up loud.

"Some station!" Bonnie said. "That's the first time I've heard 101 Strings playing '76 Trombones.'"

Glen told her that it was a tape, not the radio, and that the song was "Oklahoma!" All of Martin's tapes were instrumental—he hated vocals—but it just so happened that Glen had a tape of his own in the glove compartment, a Peter Paul and Mary. He said nothing to Bonnie about it because he didn't like her tone.

"I'm going to catch some zees," she said after a time. "If Sunshine acts cute just smack him in the face. It's the only thing he understands. I got him from a cop." She rolled up her denim jacket and propped it under her head. "Wake me up," she said, "if you see anything interesting or unusual."

The sun came up, a milky presence at Glen's right shoulder, whitening the fog but not breaking through it. Glen began to notice a rushing sound like water falling hard on pavement and realized that the road had filled up with cars. Their headlights were bleached and wan. All the drivers, including Glen, changed lanes constantly.

Glen put on "Exodus" by Ferrante and Teicher, Martin's favorite. Martin had seen the movie four times. He thought it was the greatest movie ever made because it showed what you could do if you had the will. Once in a while Martin would sit in the living room by himself with a bottle of whiskey and get falling-down drunk. When he was halfway there he would yell Glen's name until Glen came downstairs and sat with him. Then Martin would lecture him on various subjects. He often repeated himself, and one of his favorite topics was the Jewish people, which was what he called the Jews who died in the camps. He made a distinction between them and the Israelis. This was part of his theory.

According to Martin the Jewish people had done the Israelis a favor by dying out; if they had lived they would have weakened the gene pool and the Israelis would not have had the strength or the will to take all that land away from the Arabs and keep it.

One night he asked whether Glen had noticed anything that he, Martin, had in common with the Israelis. Glen admitted that he had missed the connection. The Israelis had been in exile for a long time, Martin said; he himself, while in the Navy, had visited over thirty ports of call and lived at different times in seven of the United States before coming home to Seattle. The Israelis had taken a barren land and made it fruitful; Martin had taken over a failing company and made it turn a profit again. The Israelis defeated all their enemies and Martin was annihilating his competition. The key, Martin said, was in the corporate gene pool.

You had to keep cleaning out the deadwood and bringing in new blood. Martin named the deadwood who would soon be cleaned out, and Glen was surprised; he had supposed a few of the people to be, like himself, new blood.

The fog held. The ocean spray gave it a sheen, a pearly color. Big drops of water rolled up the windshield, speckling the gray light inside the car. Glen saw that Bonnie was not a girl but a woman. She had wrinkles across her brow and in the corners of her mouth and eyes, and the streaks in her hair were real streaks— not one of these fashions as he'd first thought. In the light her skin showed its age like a coat of dust. She was old, not *old* old, but old: older than him. Glen felt himself relax, and realized that for a moment there he had been interested in her. He squinted into the fog and drove on with the sensation of falling through a cloud. Behind Glen the dog stirred and yelped in his dreams.

Bonnie woke up outside Olympia. "I'm hungry," she said, "let's score some pancakes."

Glen stopped at a Denny's. While the waitress went for their food Bonnie told Glen about a girl friend of hers, not the one in Seattle but another one, who had known the original Denny. Denny, according to her girl friend, was muy weird. He had made a proposition. He would set Bonnie's girl friend up with a place of her own, a car, clothes, the works; he wanted only one thing in return. "Guess what," Bonnie said.

"I give up," Glen said.

"All right," Bonnie said, "you'd never guess it anyway." The proposition, she explained, had this price tag: her girl friend had to invite different men over for dinner, one man at a time, at least three days a week. The restaurateur didn't care what happened after the meal, had no interest in this respect either as participant or observer. All he wanted was to sit under the table while they ate, concealed by a floor-length tablecloth.

Glen said that there had to be more to it than that.

"No sir," Bonnie said. "That was the whole proposition."

"Did she do it?" Glen asked.

Bonnie shook her head. "She already had a boy friend, she didn't need some old fart living under her table."

"I still don't get it," Glen said, "him wanting to do that. What's the point?"

"The point?" Bonnie looked at Glen as if he had said something comical. "Search me," she said. "I guess he's just into food. Some people can't leave their work at the office. This other girl friend of mine knew a mechanic and before, you know, he used to smear himself all over with grease. Can you feature that?" Bonnie went at her food—a steak, an order of pancakes, a salad and two wedges of lemon meringue pie—and did not speak again until she had eaten everything but the steak, which she wrapped in a place mat and stuck in her purse. "I have to admit," she said, "that was the worst meal I ever ate."

Glen went to the men's room and when he came out again the table was empty. Bonnie waved him over to the door. "I already paid," she said, stepping outside.

Glen followed her across the parking lot. "I was going to have some more coffee," he said.

"Well," she said, "I'll tell you straight. That wouldn't be a good idea right now."

"In other words you didn't pay."

"Not exactly."

"What do you mean, 'not exactly'?"

"I left a tip," she said. "I'm all for the working girl but I can't see paying for garbage like that. They ought to pay us for eating it. It's got cardboard in it, for one thing, not to mention about ten million chemicals."

"What's got cardboard in it?"

"The batter. Uh-oh, Sunshine's had a little accident."

Glen looked into the back seat. There was a big stain on the cover. "Godalmighty," Glen said. The dog looked at him and wagged his tail. Glen turned the car back on to the road; it was too late to go back to the restaurant, he'd never be able to explain. "I noticed," he said, "you didn't leave anything on your plate, considering it was garbage."

"If I hadn't eaten it, they would have thrown it out. They throw out pieces of butter because they're not square. You know how much food they dump every day?"

"They're running a business," Glen said. "They take a risk and they're entitled to the profits."

"I'll tell you," Bonnie said. "Enough to feed the population of San Diego. Here, Sunshine." The dog stood with his paws on the back of the seat while Bonnie shredded the steak and put the pieces in his mouth. When the steak was gone she hit the dog in the face and he sat back down.

Glen was going to ask Bonnie why she wasn't afraid of poisoning Sunshine but he was too angry to do anything but steer the car and squeeze the tennis ball. They could have been arrested back there. He could just see himself calling Martin and saying that he wouldn't be home for dinner because he was in jail for walking a check in East Jesus. Unless he could get that seat cleaned up he was going to have to tell Martin about Bonnie, and that wasn't going to be any picnic, either. So much for trying to do favors for people.

"This fog is getting to me," Bonnie said. "It's really boring." She started to say something else, then fell silent again. There was a truck just ahead of them; as they climbed a gentle rise the fog thinned and Glen could make out the logo on the back— WE MOVE FAMILIES NOT JUST FURNITURE—then they descended into the fog again and the truck vanished. "I was in a sandstorm once," Bonnie said, "in Arizona. It was really dangerous but at least it wasn't boring." She pulled a strand of hair in front of her eyes and began picking at the ends. "So," she said, "tell me about yourself."

Glen said there wasn't much to tell.

"What's your wife's name?"

"I'm not married."

"Oh yeah? Somebody like you, I thought for sure you'd be married."

"I'm engaged," Glen said. He often told strangers that. If he met them again he could always say it hadn't worked out. He'd once known a girl who probably would have married him but like Martin said, it didn't make sense to take on freight when you were traveling for speed.

Bonnie said that she had been married for the last two years to a man in Santa Barbara. "I don't mean married in the legal sense," she said. Bonnie said that when you knew someone else's head and they knew yours, that was being married. She had ceased to know his head when he left her for someone else. "He wanted to have kids," Bonnie said, "but he was afraid to with me, because I had dropped acid. He was afraid we would have a werewolf or something because of my chromosomes. I shouldn't have told him."

Glen knew that the man's reason for leaving her had nothing to do with chromosomes. He had left her because she was too old.

"I never should have told him," Bonnie said again. "I only dropped acid one time and it wasn't even fun." She made a rattling sound in her throat and put her hands up to her face. First her shoulders and then her whole body began jerking from side to side.

"All right," Glen said, "all right." He dropped the tennis ball and began patting her on the back as if she had hiccups.

Sunshine uncoiled from the back seat and came scrambling over Glen's shoulder. He knocked Glen's hand off the steering wheel as he jumped onto his lap, rooting for the ball. The car went into a broadside skid. The road was slick and the tires did not scream. Bonnie stopped jerking and stared out the window. So did Glen. They watched the fog whipping along the windshield as if they were at a movie. Then the car began to spin. When they came out of it Glen watched the yellow lines shoot away from the hood and realized that they were sliding backwards in the wrong lane of traffic. The car went on this way for a time, then it went into another spin and when it came out it was pointing in the right direction though still in the wrong lane. Not far off Glen could see weak yellow lights approaching, bobbing gently like the running lights of a ship. He took the wheel again and eased the car off the road. Moments later a convoy of logging trucks roared out of the fog, airhorns bawling; the car rocked in the turbulence of their wake.

Sunshine jumped into the back seat and lay there, whimpering. Glen and Bonnie moved into each other's arms. They just held on, saying nothing. Holding Bonnie, and being held by her, was necessary to Glen.

"I thought we were goners," Bonnie said.

"They wouldn't even have found us," Glen said. "Not even our shoes."

"I'm going to change my ways," Bonnie said.

"Me too," Glen said, and though he wasn't sure just what was wrong with his ways, he meant it.

"I feel like I've been given another chance," Bonnie said. "I'm going to pay back the money I owe, and write my mother a letter, even if she is a complete bitch. I'll be nicer to Sunshine. No more shoplifting. No more—" Just then another convoy of trucks went by and though Bonnie kept on talking Glen could not hear a word. He was thinking they should get started again.

Later, when they were back on the road, Bonnie said that she had a special feeling about Glen because of what they had just gone through. "I don't mean boy-girl feelings," she said. "I mean—do you know what I mean?"

"I know what you mean," Glen said.

"Like there's a bond," she said.

"I know," Glen said. And as a kind of celebration he got out his Peter Paul and Mary and stuck it in the tape deck.

"I don't believe it," Bonnie said. "Is that who I think it is?"

"Peter Paul and Mary," Glen said.

"That's who I thought it was," Bonnie said. "You like that stuff?"

Glen nodded. "Do you?"

"I guess they're all right. When I'm in the mood. What else have you got?"

Glen named the rest of the tapes.

"Jesus," Bonnie said. She decided that what she was really in the mood for was some peace and quiet.

By the time Glen found the address where Bonnie's girl friend lived, a transients' hotel near Pioneer Square, it had begun to rain. He waited in the car while Bonnie rang the bell. Through the window of the door behind her he saw a narrow ladder of stairs; the rain sliding down the windshield made them appear to be moving upward. A woman stuck her head out the door; she nodded constantly as she talked. When Bonnie came back her hair had separated into ropes. Her ears, large and pink, poked out between strands. She said that her girl friend was out, that she came and went at all hours.

"Where does she work?" Glen asked. "I could take you there."

"Around," Bonnie said. "You know, here and there." She looked at Glen and then out the window. "I don't want to stay with her," she said, "not really. I don't want to get caught up in all this again."

Bonnie went on talking like that, personal stuff, and Glen listened to the raindrops plunking off the roof of the car. He thought he should help Bonnie, and he wanted to. Then he imagined bringing Bonnie home to Martin and introducing them; Sunshine having accidents all over the new carpets; the three of them eating dinner while Bonnie talked, interrupting Martin, saying the kinds of things she said. Martin would die. Glen savored the thought, but he couldn't, he just couldn't.

When Bonnie finished talking, Glen explained to her that he really wanted to help out but that it wasn't possible.

"Sure," Bonnie said, and leaned back against the seat with her eyes closed.

It seemed to Glen that she did not believe him. That was ungrateful of her and he became angry. "It's true," he said.

"Hey," Bonnie said, and touched his arm.

"My roommate is allergic to dogs."

"Hey," Bonnie said again. "No problem." She got her bags out of the trunk and tied Sunshine's leash to the guitar case, then came around the car to the driver's window. "Well," she said, "I guess this is it."

"Here," Glen said, "in case you want to stay somewhere else." He put a twenty-dollar bill in her hand.

She shook her head and tried to give it back.

"Keep it," he said. "Please."

She stared at him. "Jesus," she said. "Okay, why not? The price is right." She looked up and down the street, then put the bill in her pocket. "I owe you one," she said. "You know where to find me."

"I didn't mean—" Glen said.

"Wait," Bonnie said. "Sunshine! Sunshine!"

Glen looked behind him. Sunshine was running up the street after another dog, pulling Bonnie's guitar case behind him. "Nuts," Bonnie said, and began sprinting up the sidewalk in the rain, cursing loudly. People stopped to watch, and a police car slowed down. Glen hoped that the officers hadn't noticed them together. He turned the corner and looked back. No one was following him.

A few blocks from home Glen stopped at a gas station and tried without success to clean the stain off the seat cover. On the floor of the car he found a lipstick and a clear plastic bag with two marijuana cigarettes inside, which he decided had fallen out of Bonnie's purse during the accident.

Glen knew that the cigarettes were marijuana because the ends were crimped. The two engineers he'd roomed with before moving in with Martin had smoked it every Friday night. They would pass cigarettes back and forth and comment on the quality, then turn the stereo on full blast and listen with their eyes closed, nodding in time to the music and now and then smiling and saying "Get down!" and "Go for it!" Later on they would strip the refrigerator, giggling as if the food belonged to someone else, then watch TV with the sound off and make up stupid dialogue. Glen suspected they were putting it on; he had taken puffs a couple of times and it didn't do anything for him. He almost threw the marijuana away but finally decided to hang on to it. He thought it might be valuable.

Glen could barely eat his dinner that night; he was nervous about the confession he had planned, and almost overcome by the smell of Martin's after-shave. Glen had sniffed the bottle once and the lotion was fine by itself, but for some reason it smelled like rotten eggs when Martin put it on. He didn't just use a drop or two, either; he drenched himself, slapping it all over his face and neck with the sound of applause. Finally Glen got his courage up and confessed to Martin over coffee. He had hoped that the offense of giving Bonnie a ride would be canceled out by his honesty in telling about it, but when he was finished Martin hit the roof.

For several minutes Martin spoke very abusively to Glen. It had happened before and Glen knew how to listen without hearing. When Martin ran out of abuse he began to lecture.

"Why didn't she have her own car?" he asked. "Because she's used to going places free. Some day she's going to find out that nothing's free. You could have done anything to her. *Anything.* And it would have been her fault, because she put herself in your power. When you put yourself in someone else's power you're nothing, nobody. You just have to accept what happens."

After he did the dishes Glen unpacked and sat at the window in his room. Horns were blowing across the sound. The fog was all around the house, thickening the air; the breath in his lungs made him feel slow and heavy.

He wondered what it really felt like, being high. Once Glen had gone hunting with his stepfather outside Wenatchee and while they were watching the sun come up a flight of geese skimmed the orchard behind them and passed overhead in a rush. As the geese wheeled south and crossed in front of the sunrise they called back and forth to each other with a sound like laughter, and their wings were outlined in gold. Glen had felt so good that he had forgotten his gun. Maybe it would be like that, like starting all over again.

He decided to try it; this time, instead of just a few puffs, he had two whole marijuana cigarettes all to himself. But not in his room—Martin came in all the time to get things out of the closet, plant food and stationery and so on, and he might smell it. Glen didn't want to go outside, either. There was always the chance of running into the police.

In the basement, just off the laundry room, was another smaller room where Martin kept wood for the fireplace. He wouldn't be going in there for another two or three months, when the weather turned cold. Probably the smell would wear off by that time; then again, maybe it wouldn't. What the hell, thought Glen.

He put on his windbreaker and went into the living room where Martin was building a model airplane. "I'm going out for a while," he said. "See you later." He walked down the hall and opened the front door. "So long!" he yelled, then slammed the door shut so Martin would hear, and went down the stairs into the basement.

Glen couldn't turn on the lights because then the fan would go on in the laundry room; the fan had a loud squeak and Martin might hear it. Glen felt his way along the wall and stumbled into something. He lit a match and saw an enormous pile of Martin's shirts, all of them white, waiting to be ironed. Martin only wore cotton because wash 'n wear gave him hives. Glen stepped over them into the wood room and closed the door. He sat on a log and smoked both of the marijuana cigarettes all the way down, holding in the smoke the way he'd been told. Then he waited for it to do something for him but it didn't. He was not happy. Glen stood up to leave, but at that moment the fan went on in the room outside so he sat down again.

He heard Martin set up the ironing board. Then the radio came on. Whenever the announcer said something Martin would talk back. "First the good news," the announcer said. "We're going to get a break tomorrow, fair all day with highs in the seventies." "Who cares?" Martin said. The announcer said that peace-seeking efforts had failed somewhere and Martin said, "Big deal." A planeload of athletes had been lost in a storm over the Rockies. "Tough tittie," said Martin. When the announcer said that a drug used in the treatment of cancer had been shown to cause de-mented behavior in laboratory rats, Martin laughed.

There was music. The first piece was a show tune, the second a blues number sung by a woman. Martin turned it off after a couple of verses. "I can sing better than that," he said. Substitut-ing da-da-dum for the words, he brought his voice to a controlled scream, not singing the melody but cutting across the line of it, making fun of the blues.

Glen had never heard a worse noise. It became part of the ab-solute darkness in which he sat, along with the bubbling sigh of the iron and the sulfurous odor of Martin's after-shave and the pall of smoke that filled his little room. He tried to reckon how many shirts might be in that pile. Twenty, thirty. Maybe more. It would take forever.

Maiden Voyage

Twice the horn had sounded, and twice Howard had waved and shouted dumb things at the people below; now he was tired and they still hadn't left the dock. But he waved again anyway, doing his best, when the horn went off a third time.

The boat began to glide out of its slip. Nora leaned against Howard, fanning the air with a long silk scarf. On the dock below their daughter held up a printed cardboard sign she had brought along for the occasion: HAPPY GOLDEN ANNIVERSARY MOM AND DAD. As the boat picked up speed she dropped the sign and kept pace beside the hull, running and yelling up at them with her hands cupped in front of her mouth. Howard worried. She had been a stupid girl and now she was a stupid woman, perfectly capable of running off the end of the pier. But she stopped finally, and grew smaller and smaller until Howard could barely make her out from the rest of the crowd. He stopped waving and turned to Nora. "I'm cold. Look at that sky. You said it was going to be warm."

Nora glanced up at the clouds. They were steely gray like the water below. "The brochure said this was an ideal time of year in these waters. Those were the exact words."

"These waters my foot." Howard gave her the look. The look was enough now, he didn't have to say anything else. Howard walked toward the steps leading to their cabin. Nora followed, quoting from the brochure.

Paper banners hung from wall to wall: "Welcome Aboard the William S. Friedman," "Happy Sailing—To Those in the Throes of Love from Those in the Business of Love." The cabin was bright with fruit and flowers; on the door hung two interlocking life preservers in the shape of hearts.

"Help me to the bathroom, Howard. I'm afraid to walk the way the floor keeps tilting."

"You don't have your sea legs yet." Howard took Nora's arm and led her to the door in the corner. "This is the head. And the floor is called the deck. If we have to be on this boat for a week you might just as well get it right." He closed the door behind her and stared around the cabin.

There was a big brass latch on the wall. Howard jiggled it and finally slipped it free and the bed fell out on top of him. It took him by surprise and almost knocked him down but he kept his footing and managed to push the bed back into the wall. Then he read the barometer and opened and closed the drawers. The upper drawers contained several bars of soap in miniature packets. Howard slipped a few in his pocket and opened the porthole and stuck his head out. Other people had their heads stuck out too. He battened the porthole and read the barometer again, then picked up the intercom.

"Testing," he said. "One two three four testing. Night Raider this is Black Hawk. Testing."

A voice crackled from the speaker. "Steward here."

"It's me. Howard. Just testing. Over and out."

Nora came back into the cabin and made her way to the couch. "It's too small in there. I couldn't breathe."

"I could have told you this wouldn't be any palace."

"I feel awful. I bet I look awful too."

Nora's face had gone white. The burst veins in her cheeks and along her upper lip stood out like notations on a map. Her eyes glittered feverishly behind her spectacles. Sick, she looked more than ever like Harry Truman, for whom Howard had not voted.

He sat beside Nora and took her hand. "You look all right."

"Do I really?"

"What'd I just say?" He let go of her hand. "Why do you always think about what you look like?"

"That's not true. I don't."

Howard paced the cabin. "Goddam boat."

"I thought it would be nice, just the two of us."

A knock came at the door and a man stuck his head in, a large square head divided by a pencil-line moustache. "Our Golden Couple," he said, smiling. "I'm Bill Tweed, your social director." His body followed his head into the cabin. "I want to extend a real warm welcome aboard from all of us here on the *Friedman*. I guess you know this is our maiden voyage. Ever been to sea?"

Howard nodded. "World War I. Before your time, I guess." He gestured toward the porthole. "You could have walked all the way from New York to Paris on top of German submarines. They got three of our ships. Saw it myself." Howard had been sure they would get him too. He had been sure of it all the way across and never slept at night for knowing it. When the war ended and he got on another ship to come back home he knew that somewhere out there was a German who hadn't gotten the word. His German. Howard had a sense of things catching up with him.

Tweed handed Howard a pamphlet. "We here on the *Friedman* feel that our business is your pleasure. Just read this over and let us know what you're interested in. We have a number of special programs for our senior sailors. Can you both walk?"

Howard just stared. "Yes," Nora said.

"Wonderful. That's a real help." He ran his forefinger across his moustache and made a notation against his clipboard. "A few more questions. Your age, Mr. Lewis?"

"I was seventy-five years old on April first. April Fool's Day."

"'Young,' Dad—seventy-five years young. We here on board the *Friedman* don't know the word 'old.' We don't believe in it. Just think of yourself as three twenty-five-year-olds. And you, Mrs. Lewis?"

"I'm seventy-eight."

"Ah. December—May. Any children?"

"Two. Sharon and Clifford."

"The poor man's riches. Happy the man who has his quiver full of them. Their occupations?"

Howard handed Nora the pamphlet. "Sharon's retarded and Clifford is in jail."

Tweed, still scribbling, looked up from the clipboard. "I'm so sorry. Of course this is all confidential."

Nora scowled at Howard. "Are you married, Mr. Tweed?"

"Indeed I am. Married to the single life. My mother keeps telling me I should take a wife but I haven't decided yet whose wife I'm going to take." He winked at Howard and pocketed his pen. "Well, then, until dinner. You'll be interested to know who your tablemates will be." He smiled secretively. "Ron and Stella Speroni. Newlyweds from Delaware. Ever been to Delaware?"

"On the train once," said Howard. "Didn't get off."

"A real nice state. Intimate. Anyway, I'm sure that Ron and Stella can learn a lot about love from you, seeing you've piled up a hundred years of it between you." Smiling at his arithmetic he closed the door.

"Whatever gave you that idea?" said Nora. "Telling him Clifford was in jail."

Howard spent most of the dinner talking to Ron. Ron reminded him of a horse. He had a long face and muddy brown eyes and when he laughed his upper lip curled up over his teeth. He

worked in his father's jewelry store in Wilmington. They specialized in synthetic diamonds and Ron was willing to bet that Howard couldn't tell the difference between their product and the
real McCoy. He had Stella take off the tiara she wore, an intricate
silver band dense with stones, and handed it to Howard.

"Go on," he said. "If you can tell the difference you can have
it." He waited, smiling at Nora and Stella.

Howard turned the tiara over a couple of times, then scraped it
along the side of a water glass.

"No fair," Ron said, snatching it away. "I already told you it was
synthetic." He stared at his wife constantly as he talked. Stella
had platinum hair going brown at the roots and long black fingernails. She didn't say much; most of the time she sat with her
chin cupped in her hand, gazing around at the other tables and
scraping her fingernails back and forth over the linen tablecloth.
Ron had met her in the shop. She came in to have some earrings
converted and one thing led to another. "She's an incredible person," Ron whispered. "You ought to see her with kids."

After dinner the waiters moved all the tables out of the center
of the room and the band started to warm up. Tweed walked out
to the middle of the dance floor holding a microphone attached
to a long wire. The room fell silent.

"Tonight," Tweed said, "we have with us what you might call
the summer and winter, the Alpha and Omega of human love.
Let's hear it for Ron and Stella Speroni, married three days this
very afternoon, and for Mom and Dad Lewis, who celebrated
their Golden Anniversary last Wednesday." Everyone clapped.

"We here on the *Friedman* have a special place for our senior
sailors. To those who are afraid of time I say: what tastes better than
old wine or old cheese? And where the art of love is concerned
(Tweed paused) we all know that old wood gives off the most
heat." Everyone laughed. Nora sent a smile around the room.
Howard cracked his knuckles under the table. Stella grinned at
him and he looked away. Then Ron and Nora and Stella all stood

together and he stood too and found himself dancing with Stella. He held her awkwardly as the music began, not knowing what to say and not wanting to look down at all the faces looking up at him.

Stella spoke first. "You've got strong hands."

"I used to do a lot of lifting."

Stella raised his hand and opened it and ran a black fingernail across his palm. "You're very passionate. Look." She traced a crease running from his wrist to the base of his forefinger.

"Probably comes from my grandfather. He had fourteen kids. He was still grinding them out in his sixties."

"I have the same thing." Stella showed him her own palm. Her scent was overwhelming. "When were you born?"

"April first. April Fool's Day."

"Aries." Stella grinned. "The Ram." Howard could see the dank glimmer of gold in her back teeth.

"I don't know about any rams. I guess I do all right."

"People like us shouldn't get married. We have too much passion for just one person."

"Marrying Nora was the smartest thing I ever did."

"Ron and I have an open marriage."

Howard turned this over for a moment. He felt adventurous. "So do me and Nora."

"Wow, think of that." Stella stepped backwards. "You were ahead of your time. You really were."

"Well, like the man says—you only live once."

"Me and Ron figure that's the best way of dealing with the problem. You know, instead of sneaking around and all that stuff. Ron is very understanding."

The music stopped and everyone applauded and Howard led Stella back to the table. He and Nora watched people dance for a while but she wouldn't talk to him and he could tell she was mad about something. Finally she got up and walked outside. He followed and stood silently beside her, leaning against the rail.

The rolling swells had flattened out but a mist had fallen over the ship like a screen. Howard reached out and touched Nora's arm. She stiffened.

"Don't touch me."

Howard drew his arm back.

"I know who you're thinking about," Nora said.

"All right. Who am I thinking about?"

"Miriam Selby."

Howard stared over the side of the ship. "She does look like Miriam, I'll grant you. Can't see where that's any fault of mine."

"You don't love me. You never have."

"There you are," said a voice behind them. "Sneaking off already, eh? And unchaperoned. We'll have to see about this." Tweed stepped closer. "How did you get on with the Speronis?"

"Nice couple," Nora said. "Attractive."

"Youth." Tweed shook his head. "A once-in-a-lifetime experience. I just wanted to remind you about the costume party tomorrow night."

"But we don't have any costumes."

"Don't worry, Mom. We provide everything. Well then. You two behave yourselves."

Howard leaned against the rail, watching Tweed move along the deck until he disappeared into the mist.

"Howard, I'm sorry."

He took Nora's hand.

"Do you love me?" she said.

"Sure. Sure I do."

"You never say so." Nora waited but Howard didn't answer. "It's all right," she said, leaning against him; "it doesn't matter." Howard put his arm around her and stared down over the railing, watching the water, black as oil, slide along the hull of the boat.

When the horn gave the alarm—HAHOOGA HAHOOGA HAHOOGA—Howard came awake knowing that his German had found him. He accepted it without bitterness, even with some self-satisfaction. He had, after all, been right.

Nora sat up, the covers pulled around her throat. "Howard, what is it?"

"Submarine." Howard got out of bed and put on his robe and went out into the companionway. The passage was choked with people asking each other what the horn meant. Just then one of the ship's attendants came through and told everyone not to worry and to go back to bed. Someone had brought a hot plate aboard and left it plugged in and it had started a small fire. Howard was about to go back in the cabin when Ron Speroni came up to him. He wore pajama tops over striped tuxedo trousers.

"Excuse me, Mr. Lewis. Have you seen Stella?"

"No. Why?"

"I just thought maybe you had."

"You share the same cabin, don't you?"

Speroni nodded. "She went up on deck for some fresh air. When I woke up after that whistle went off she still wasn't back."

"When did she go out?"

"About eleven."

"That was three hours ago."

"I know." Speroni looked down at his bare feet. His toes were long and hairy and curled like a monkey's. Howard decided to help him.

"Let's take a look around. Maybe she fell asleep up on deck."

They went topside and walked along the rail, peering at the rows of empty deck chairs by the misty glow of the running lights. Then, as they approached the stern, a man's voice came to them, fruity, disembodied, chuckling portentously. They looked around. They saw nothing. Then came the woman's voice, murmuring and low, suddenly breaking into laughter unmistakably Stella's.

The voices came from the lifeboat hanging across the stern. Speroni leaned forward, trembling slightly, his arms rigid at his sides, his eyes fixed on the darkness above the boat. Howard reached out and took him by the elbow. Speroni turned to him, his mouth twitching, and Howard felt him yield. He walked Speroni around the bow to the other side of the boat. Under the lights Speroni's cheeks shone like wet pavement. Howard looked out over the water.

"She didn't fall overboard," Speroni said. "She's safe. That's the main thing."

Howard nodded.

"Don't get the wrong idea. Stella's very moral, really."

"I'm sure she is."

"You ought to see her with kids."

"I was thinking," Howard said, "maybe this is a stage she's going through."

"Maybe." Speroni rubbed at his eyes with the back of his sleeve. "I'm cold. Coming down?"

"Later. You go on ahead."

Speroni took a couple of steps, then turned. "You really think this is a stage she's going through?"

"Could be."

"That's what I think, too. I just wouldn't want you to get the wrong impression. Stella's a beautiful person. Very spiritual."

The mist was lifting. A few stars began to appear, blinking remotely. Howard wondered what Aries looked like. He heard voices and footsteps and Stella's laugh and looked up. "Hello, Stella. Mr. Tweed."

Tweed looked up and down the deck. "Evening, Dad. Stargazing, are you? We're never too old for dreams." He held his watch up to his face. "It's late," he said. "I'll wish you goodnight."

"Hi, Howard." Stella leaned on the railing. "Bill's a real card but a little bit of him goes a long way, if you know what I mean. So what brings you up here at this hour?"

"Just getting some fresh air."

"Look—the stars are out. Don't you wish you could reach out and pick them like flowers?"

"I hadn't thought of it."

"Life. That's the way life is to me, Howard. You keep picking things until you get the one thing that really matters. Tell me about your great love."

"My great love?"

"How did you meet her?" Stella did a pirouette, one hand held aloft. "Was it at a dance? What was she wearing?"

"Me and Nora were friends since we were kids."

"Not Nora, Howard. She's your wife."

"That's what I'm saying."

"Come on, Howard. Anyone can see she's not your great love. What did she look like, Howard?"

Howard glanced at Stella, then stared back over the railing. "Nora's been good to me. Marrying Nora was the smartest thing I ever did."

"What did she call you, Howard?"

"It don't last, the other thing. You can't trust it."

"What did she call you?"

Howard scratched his wrist. "Sunshine."

"Sunshine. That's beautiful, Howard. That's really beautiful. I'll bet that's what you were, too. Just for her."

"You can't trust it."

"So what? What else is there?"

"There's a lot else. A lot."

"But what?"

"Don't you think you ought to be with Ron instead of tearing around up here? There's certain considerations, you know, like people's feelings."

"Considerations? No thanks, Howard. That's what they make cages out of." Stella stepped back and gave Howard's arm a friendly squeeze. "Don't you go and get stuffy on me, now I know you."

Howard went to the costume party as a buccaneer. A sort of gentleman pirate. Actually the costume was that of an eighteenth century squire—ruffled shirt front, brocade jacket, and knee pants with buckled shoes—but Nora had made him an eyepatch and Tweed lent him the captain's ceremonial sword. Nora came as Venus. She wore a flowing toga and Tweed gave her some plastic leaves to weave into her hair. He said they gave the costume a Greek accent.

They had their own table. The Speronis sat across the room, Stella wearing her tiara and below it a low-cut peasant girl's smock with billowing sleeves. Ron had on a Confederate officer's uniform from the Civil War. He looked unhappy.

After dinner the room went dark. A few moments later red shafts of light shot out from the corners and began moving over the dance floor. Someone played a long mounting roll on a snare drum. A white spotlight blazed out on the middle of the floor and Tweed stepped into it.

"Friends, before we go any further I just wonder if we couldn't all take a moment and think about why we're here. I'm not talking about old Sol up there, who was kind enough to come out and give us a big smile today. I'm not even talking about our excellent cuisine, painstakingly prepared for us courtesy of Monsieur and Madame Grimes."

The spotlight moved over to the door of the kitchen. The cooks waved and smiled and the spotlight raced back to Tweed, who held up his arms for silence. The spotlight jerked to the right and Tweed sidestepped back into focus. "I'm talking about what really brings us here—I'm talking about love. That's right, love. A word you don't hear much these days but I for one am not ashamed to say it—and to say it again—LOVE! And I'll bet you're not either. L-O-V-E—LOVE!"

A few people joined in. "Love," they said.

"All together! Come on now, let them hear you all the way back home. L-O-V-E—"

"LOVE!" everyone shouted.

"Now your hearts are talking. That's it—love, the artillery of heaven. We here on the *Friedman* like to believe that love still calls the shots in this battered and bruised old world of ours. And we think we can prove it. Because if two individuals can stack up a century of love between them, well, as far as I personally am concerned the smartalecks will just have to go home and think of something else to try and make us give up on. Because we're sure as heck not going to give up on love. You know who I'm talking about. Let's hear it for Mom and Dad Lewis. Let's hear it for a hundred years of love!"

The sound of clapping filled the room. Howard covered his unpatched eye as it filled with hot silver light. Someone was tugging at his arm.

"Stand up!" Nora hissed.

Howard stood up. Nora was smiling and bowing, the green plastic leaves in her hair bobbing up and down. Howard groped behind him for his chair but Nora clamped down even harder on his arm.

The spotlight returned to Tweed. "Maybe we can persuade these two fine individuals to say a word to us. How about it, Mom and Dad? How did you do it?"

Howard shrank back but Nora pulled him along. He let her lead him to the middle of the room, unsettled by her forcefulness.

Nora took the microphone. She smiled, her spectacles glittering in the spotlight: "Girls, don't ever let yourselves get run down and go to pieces. A little exercise every day. Don't ever let the sun set on a quarrel." She chuckled and looked at Howard. "And don't be afraid to stand up and give your man what for every once in a while." She ducked her head at the applause.

Howard took the microphone. He stared at it as if it were something he was being asked to eat. "Nothing to it," he said. "You just go from day to day and before you know it fifty years are up." He tried to think of something else to say but he couldn't. That was all there was. He frowned at the microphone, the silence building as it dropped slowly to his side.

Tweed started another round of clapping. "Thank you," he said, retrieving the microphone. He nodded in the direction of the bandstand. A single clarinet began to play "The Anniversary Waltz." The spotlight mellowed.

Howard understood that he was expected to dance with Nora. As he took her hand the boat plunged into a swell and the deck pitched. Nora stumbled but caught herself. Howard thought they should probably be talking to each other.

"You're getting your sea legs," he said.

Nora moved close to him, pressed her cheek to his. The plastic leaves crinkled against his forehead. His unpatched eye ached. Howard turned slowly around to escape Stella's grin, and above it, the winking of her tiara in the moving red light.

Worldly Goods

Davis and his dinner partner were waiting for a taxi one night when she saw a pinball arcade across the street. She insisted they play a few games before going home and when Davis reminded her that it was getting late she said, "Oh, don't be such an old fuddy-duddy." Though he did not see the woman again, that remark bothered him.

Not long afterwards he was looking at secondhand cars and saw, in the back of the lot, a powerful automobile just like one his best friend had owned when they were boys; the same make, even the same year. The salesman admired it with Davis for a moment, then tried to interest him in a newer car, an ugly gray sedan with lots of trunk room. Suddenly Davis felt angry. He went back to the first car, worked the gears for a while, then bought it and drove it home.

That Saturday Davis took the car out to Long Island. On the highway he passed a similar model, a few years older, and he and the other driver honked at each other.

The next morning Davis decided to show the car to some peo-

ple he knew from back home. He had been an usher at their wedding, and when he first came to town he had stayed with them for
a few months while he was looking for a place of his own.

There was a peep-hole in the door and after Davis rang the
bell he smiled at it. He heard whispers. "I wish you'd call," the
husband said as he opened the door.

The apartment smelled sour, and dirty ashtrays were stacked
on the end tables next to half-empty glasses with limp slices of
lemon floating in them. The husband was mute, the wife ner-
vously chatty. Davis wondered why they had not invited him to
the party. Then he thought of something he had forgotten: when
the wife's father died two years earlier they'd left for Shreveport
without saying good-bye.

"I bought a car," Davis said.

"You're kidding," the wife said. "I didn't even know you could
drive."

"It's right outside," Davis said.

They laughed when they saw it. The husband stood on the
sidewalk with his arms folded, smiling and shaking his head. "Hot
dog!" said the wife. "If anybody else told me this baby belonged to
you I would never believe them. Not in a million years."

Before long Davis began to wish he hadn't bought the car. It
was not in good condition. Patches of rust showed through the
paint, and the engine was filthy and out of phase. Gasoline went
through it like pork through a duck. Richie, the boy across the
street, offered to fix it up but Davis thought that he had already
carried things far enough. "I'll think about it," he said, really in-
tending to drive the car the way it was until it fell apart.

Soon after he bought the car Davis collided with a Japanese
compact. He had been moving forward and the compact had
been backing up. The cars came together with an awful grinding
sound. Davis had seen few women as tall as the one who emerged

from the compact, and as she uncoiled from her seat he had the sense of watching a biological process.

Together they circled the cars. His, tanklike, had bellied up on her trunk, folding it like an accordion. She had punched out his headlight and crumpled his right fender. "I should have stayed home today," the woman said, "and I would have, too, if it wasn't for my business." She was wearing yellow designer sunglasses and her hair was covered with a yellow scarf. She had bony wrists and her knees, fully exposed beneath the hem of her blue dress, were also bony. As she spoke she chipped away methodically at a ridge of paint on the trunk of the compact, using her fingernails like tools. "I'll probably get all the blame," she said. "You know how they always talk about women drivers."

"Don't worry," Davis said, "it wasn't all your fault. I should have been paying closer attention."

"Oh, but they'll claim it's my fault in the end," she said bitterly.

Davis thought that one of them should call the police; perhaps they could make some assignment of guilt. He called from a grocery store, watching the woman as he talked. She sat in his car, crying. When he joined her again Davis tried to comfort her by pointing out that though her car was damaged she herself was not. "That's the important thing," he said.

"Not to my husband." She looked at her watch. "I can't wait any longer."

"The police should be here soon."

"But I have a business meeting. I mustn't be late. I *can't* be late."

"We really should be here when the police come," Davis said. Then, thinking her business meeting a fabrication, he added: "There's nothing to be afraid of."

"My husband beats me," she said, "when I don't make enough money." She insisted that it was not necessary for both of them to wait for the police, that they had only to report the accident to their insurance companies. Finally Davis agreed, and they exchanged names and license numbers. Before the woman left she gave Davis a brochure with her card attached. He backed his machine off hers and she drove away, tires squealing under the pressure of collapsed metal. Davis glanced through the brochure while he waited for the police. "Clara!" it said on the cover: "Concepts For Spacious Living." There was a picture of a woman, not Clara, sitting in a chrome chair on an Oriental rug in the middle of an otherwise empty barn.

The claims adjuster wore a silver whistle around his neck. When he noticed Davis staring at it he explained that it was for muggers. "Last month alone," he said, "there were three robberies on my street. Incidents is what the police call them, but you lose your money just the same. I don't know, maybe it's all this busing—the you-know-whats are taking over. But here I am telling you, a Southerner. You have personally seen all this yourself."

Davis did not take to the suggestion that he had anything in common with this man, or to the implication that by virtue of being from the South he was bound to extend hospitality to other people's hatreds. "I wouldn't know," he said. "I've been here a long time."

"Far be it from me to cast racial slurs," the adjuster said. "You don't have to tell me where that leads to. Not a day goes by that I don't say 'Live and let live!' But these people will take your wallet and shoot you in the head." The adjuster leaned forward. "I see that I am offending you. Forgive me. But when I walk in the street at night I hear noises where there aren't any. That's why I said those things. Fear. I admit it, I'm afraid."

Davis recited the facts of the accident and the adjuster took them down on a form, writing in long, rhythmic strokes. Davis read the cartoons under the glass desk top while he waited for the adjuster to catch up. In one cartoon the judge was questioning a woman with her arm in a sling. "How far," the judge asked, "have you been able to raise your arm since the accident?" Frowning with pain, the woman raised her hand shoulder-high. "And how far could you raise it *before* the accident?" Brightly she held her hand above her head. Another cartoon showed three gypsies leaning together and shedding tears while the one in the middle sawed at a violin. "Oh, *do* tell us your story!" the caption said.

"This is good," the adjuster said when Davis had finished. "This is very good. If they get funny we will eat them alive." He pushed a card across the desk. "Here is our doctor. The sooner you see him the better."

"I have my own doctor. Anyway I feel fine. We didn't really crash, just sort of bumped."

"Today you feel fine, okay. But what about next year? I have seen a lot of cervical sprain in my time and I can tell you it is no laughing matter."

"You mean whiplash?"

"Cervical sprain is I believe what they say in the medical business."

Davis would never be able to claim that he had whiplash. It was too public. People made jokes about it. "I feel fine," he said again, and pushed the card back. The adjuster put it away with a shrug and gave Davis the report to sign. Davis read it through, shaking his head. "You've completely twisted my words around," he said. "You make it seem like a hit-and-run."

"Show me where I said hit-and-run. I did not say any such thing. You told me she left the scene of the accident and that is what I said, no more."

"But I told her she could leave."

"You told her she could leave. Oh boy. I don't care what you told her, she should not have left the scene of the accident and that is the whole point."

"I know what you want," Davis said. "You want to throw the blame on her so the other company has to pay everything."

"No!" the adjuster said. "I am only trying to protect you. Maybe she will try to make money out of this—it happens every day."

"You even make it sound as if the accident were her fault."

"You were driving at a lawful rate of speed and she backed into you is what I have there. Legally speaking she is at fault."

"All I want," Davis said, "is for you to write down what happened the way I tell it to you. I was there and you weren't."

The adjuster shook his head and sighed as he made up the new form. "Terrible," he said. "This leaves you with no protection."

Davis signed it and handed it back. "That's all right. It's the truth."

"Maybe, but I know a mistake when I see one. So be it. We will need two estimates."

Davis was going into a drugstore a block from the insurance company when he heard someone calling him. It was the adjuster. He had been running. His face was streaming and the whistle bounced on his chest. He looked like a coach. "Listen," he said, "I've been thinking maybe I insulted you."

"You didn't insult me."

"Then let me buy you a cup of coffee. Or a Coke, whatever."

Davis was not due at work for another half hour, and simply did not have the energy to lie to the man. So he sat at the counter and sipped an iced tea and listened to the adjuster tell about the Southern friends he had had in the Marine Corps. It surprised Davis to hear that he had been a Marine, and he probably wouldn't have believed it if the adjuster had not taken from his wallet several photographs and spread them across the countertop.

"This is Johnny Lee," the adjuster said, stabbing his finger at one of the soldiers in a group picture. "Related to the great general, Robert E. Lee. Every night we would sit up, the two of us, and talk about life. We had different philosophies but we were like brothers." He put the photographs away, looking hard at each one as he did so.

Davis's tea was empty but he pulled on the straw, making a commotion so the adjuster would know he was ready to leave.

"What happened in the office today," the adjuster said, "I was doing my job, I was trying to help."

"I understand that," Davis said, standing up. Together they walked outside.

"It wasn't lies," the adjuster said, "not the way you thought. That is how we make out an accident report—for protection. But I know you don't see it like that. You are a Southern gentleman."

"I was brought up in the South."

"Down there you have all that tradition. Honor. Up here—" he swept his hand around—"all they know is grab. I tell you, it is hard to be a good man. Well," the adjuster stepped back, "I won't detain you." He said this in a formal way and gave a slight bow which he evidently thought to be courtly. Davis attributed the gesture to some movie the adjuster had seen with belles and gallants and pillared houses.

A man who worked with Davis recommended Leo the Lion so he took the car there for an estimate. Leo the Lion was a perfectly made, very small man. His mechanic's overalls were tailored to nip in at the waist and flare at the legs. His top two buttons were undone. He paid no attention to Davis when Davis told him that all he wanted was the dents pounded out and the headlight replaced. Instead he made Davis get down and look at the underside of the fender. It was crusted and black. There were wires everywhere. Davis tugged at his trousers, trying to keep the cuffs off the floor.

"See?" Leo the Lion said. "The metal's just about rusted through. We start banging on that and it'll fall apart." He turned and walked toward his office. Davis got to his feet and followed. There was a lion painted in velvet over the desk. A large stuffed lion was seated on one of the chairs and another peered out from behind the dusty leaves of a philodendron.

Leo the Lion took several manuals down from the shelves and made calculations. He showed them to Davis.

"Nine hundred dollars," Davis said. "That seems very high. Why do you have to repaint the whole car?"

"Because when we find another fender it's going to be a different color. We can't match the color you've got, they don't make it any more. That's why." He put the manuals away. Then he explained to Davis that he might not be able to do the job at all. Cars like that were rare and it wouldn't be easy to locate a fender for it. But he had access to a computer which was plugged in to salvage yards all over the country, so if anybody could do it he could.

"Nine hundred dollars," Davis said.

"You can probably get it done cheaper if you look around," Leo the Lion said. "I wouldn't vouch for the work, though. That car's cherry except for the fender. It's a classic. People are investing in classics these days. They put them on blocks and run the engine once a week, then take them to rallies."

Davis folded the estimate sheet and said that he would be in touch, thinking that no way was he going to spend nine hundred dollars getting a fender fixed. As he drove away he saw another shop up the street and took the car in there. The mechanic told him it wasn't worth the trouble and offered to take it off his hands for three hundred dollars.

"It's worth more than that," Davis said. "How much to fix it?"

"Twelve hundred dollars."

"That's a lot of money."

The mechanic laughed. He monkeyed around with the figures and brought the total down to a thousand. He explained the difficulties he would have repairing the car. "Oh, all right," he said suddenly, as though Davis had been trying to beat him down, and made up another estimate for seven hundred dollars. "That's my absolute bottom price," he said. "I can't do it for less and come out ahead."

As Davis was leaving the shop the mechanic ran toward the car, waving a piece of paper. Davis assumed that he had come up with another set of figures. "You forgot this," the mechanic said, and pushed the first estimate through the window. Seeing that Davis did not understand, he explained how Davis could make himself an easy five hundred. He spoke with an angry kind of patience, the way people back home spoke to Negroes who couldn't follow simple instructions. Davis was furious. He crumpled the paper and threw it out the window. For a time he considered reporting the man to an appropriate agency but decided against it. He would look like a whiner, and anyway he had no real proof.

A few days later the adjuster called Davis at work. "I trust this is not a busy time for you," he said.

Actually this was the busiest part of the day, but Davis did not wish to seem rude so he said nothing.

"Hello?" the adjuster said.

"I'm here," Davis said. "Did you get the estimates?"

"I did indeed receive your estimates only yesterday by the mail."

"They seemed high to me. If you like I'll get some more. I'm sure I can do better."

The adjuster was not calling about the estimates. A more important matter had come up which he thought he should not discuss over the telephone. Davis agreed to drop in later. When he hung up his mouth was dry and his pulse racing. He knew that guilty people felt like this and decided to have the adjuster withdraw his claim that very day.

"That will not be possible at this time," the adjuster said when Davis advised him of his intentions. "This woman has filed a claim against you which if she wins is going to cost a lot." He slid a form across the desk and when Davis had read it he asked, "Do you understand?"

"No."

"What she is saying is you ran into her because you were not watching where you were going and also you were driving at an illegal rate of speed."

"But that's not true!"

"She is claiming three thousand dollars in damages."

Davis thought that was absurd, but the adjuster did not find it so. "She is not saying anything about personal injury, thank God. It would be a mess. I could tell you stories."

Davis closed his eyes.

"She is saying you told her, quote unquote: 'Don't worry, it wasn't your fault, I wasn't paying attention.'" The adjuster looked over the top of the paper. "Which is a complete falsehood of course."

"Not exactly."

The adjuster lowered the paper. "You told her this?"

"Not those exact words," Davis said. "It meant nothing, I was just being polite." He looked down at the desk, at a cartoon of a man standing in front of a jury and displaying an empty sleeve where his right arm should have been. From behind, the outline of his missing arm was clear beneath the jacket, and his hand poked out below. "That's the truth," Davis said.

"Polite! Oh boy!" The adjuster laughed, then stopped and peered closely at Davis. "Forgive me," he said, "but you don't look so hot. You feel okay? You want some water?"

"I'm all right," Davis said.

"Come on, I'll buy you an iced tea. The other day I talked, now it's your turn."

"I have to get back to work," Davis said. "What are we going to do?"

"What I told you before. You say she backed up without looking and hit you and left the scene of the accident. None of this stuff about you told her she could go. No more polite. This is time for impolite."

"That would contradict the first report I gave you."

"What report?" The adjuster took a form out of his desk and began tearing it into long shreds. "What report?" he repeated.

"You didn't turn it in?"

"You want a miracle? You want me to turn in what does not exist? So—you have a sense of humor, you're smiling."

Richie, the boy from across the street, came over with a friend. "I can fix that light for you," he said. "Fifty dollars. It won't look like much but you'll be legal." His friend stood behind him staring at the car. Rust was gathering in the folds of the metal. "Thirty for the light," said Richie, "twenty for labor." The boy with him suddenly flipped over on his back and crawled under the car.

"I don't know," Davis said. "I'm considering having it done right."

"That'll cost you. It's not going to be easy, finding parts for this, but I guess you won't have to sweat the bucks, you can put the screws to your insurance company. It'd be worth it, fixing this car up. I can do it if you want. I'll give you a good price."

Davis could see nothing of the boy under the car except the soles of his shoes. One was brown and the other was black. His feet made a V, reminding Davis of pictures he had seen of dead soldiers. He had no idea what the boy could be doing under there. "I'll take it into consideration," Davis said.

Richie kicked his friend's shoes and the boy rolled out from underneath the car. "I can give you an estimate," Richie said importantly. "Just let me know."

"Where are you going to find the parts?"

Richie and his friend looked at each other and grinned.

Davis tried to read after dinner that night but the story made no sense to him. He could not understand why the people did what they did or said what they said. Finally he decided to visit his friends from home.

They were doing the dishes when Davis arrived. He watched

TV in the living room and when they joined him he told them all about the accident, about Clara and the adjuster and the crooked mechanic. What should he do?

The wife yawned. "Search me," she said. "I've never been in an accident."

She went to bed and her husband got up and began tidying the room. "I'm not impressed with this display of virtue," he said. "If you really want to do something worthwhile why didn't you help us with the dishes? In the five months you stayed here with us you never once offered to wash the dishes."

He followed Davis to the door. "Nothing is good enough for you," he said. "When you were looking at apartments they were always too big or small, too far from work or too close to the traffic. It doesn't take anybody five months to find an apartment. And when we took you to parties you acted bored and left early. Oh, what the hell. I'm sorry!" He shouted down the stairs: "Call me tomorrow!"

The thing to do, Davis thought, was to sit down and reason with Clara. She had seemed ridiculous to him but not dishonest. Probably her adjuster had gotten to her, or her husband. He could imagine how someone like her might get confused trying to do both the right thing and the pleasing thing.

He considered calling Clara, but her husband might answer and hang up, a strange man asking for his wife. Davis knew that somewhere there was someone capable of jealousy over Clara, and it was just possible that she had married him. Finally he copied down the address from the brochure and drove there.

Davis parked across the street. The houses in this neighborhood were very expensive, which irritated him. What could people like that, who could afford to live in such a house, possibly want with another three thousand dollars?

A long shadow passed across the drapes in the front window. It might have been Clara or it might have been her husband. To marry someone as tall as Clara, and beat her, you would have to be big—really big. But it was not this consideration that kept Davis in his car. He was thinking that he shouldn't go around like a child, without keeping his eyes open, without thinking twice about everything. He ought to have learned that by now. If he got out of his car and went up to Clara's door, they would find a way of using his honesty against him as they had used his good manners against him. He pitied her and he pitied himself.

Oh Clara, he thought, why can't we tell the truth?

After Davis got the check he took the car down to Leo the Lion. The other man was cheaper but Davis thought he would cut corners. Richie was too young and inexperienced and probably wouldn't have the right tools. Davis did not care for the way Leo the Lion swaggered but he took it as a sign of pride, and in his experience proud people did good work. And the computer thing impressed him. When a mechanic got involved with computers, my God, that showed he was serious about fixing cars.

When Davis went down to pick it up he was surprised at how beautiful the car was. People on the shop floor whistled when Leo the Lion drove it up from the basement parking lot. The color was brighter than Davis had thought from the sample book, brighter than he would have wished, but everyone else seemed to like it.

"The lock on the passenger side is broken," Leo the Lion said. "The brakes aren't good for more than another five thousand miles. She runs fine, though." He sent Davis off with a small stuffed lion and a bumper sticker—"Treat Yourself to a Leo Today."

The motor had been cleaned and fine-tuned, and Davis noticed the difference immediately. The car was faster, more responsive. The engine made a throaty, bubbling sound and banged like a pistol whenever he down-shifted. On his way home a bunch of boys pulled up next to Davis at a red light. Their car had wide tires and was raised in back. The driver gunned his engine several times. Davis fed his own engine a little gas to keep it turning over and it popped loudly. The boys started yelling things at him, not mean but playful. Davis stared straight ahead. When the light changed the other car laid rubber, and the boys in the back seat grinned over their shoulders at him.

The adjuster called one last time. He called Davis at home, and Davis resented it. "Listen," the adjuster said, "I am very intuitive and I have this picture of you brooding all the time. You have to remember that up here is different from down there. Down there you can do things right. You have honor, what you call the gentleman code."

"It's the same there as here," Davis said. "It's no different anywhere."

"You got scrunched," the adjuster said, "and you got paid for getting scrunched, which seems to me fair."

"I agree," Davis said.

"Which also calls for a celebration," the adjuster said, who then astonished Davis by inviting him to dinner on the following Wednesday. "You will like my wife," said the adjuster. "She is very interesting with a degree in music. Do you enjoy music?"

"Not especially," Davis said, though he did.

"No matter. With my wife you can talk about anything and she can talk right back. She cooks the old way. In twenty years cooking like this will be a memory, only a memory."

Davis thought that he could very well imagine the kinds of things he would be expected to put in his mouth. He told the adjuster that he was busy on Wednesday and when the adjuster suggested Thursday, he said that he was busy that night as well. "You will find that my wife and me are flexible," the adjuster said. "Whatever day will be fine with us. You name it. You say when."

Davis could not speak. The silence gathered and he could not think of anything to say to break it with.

"Correct me," the adjuster said, "but maybe you would rather not come."

Davis switched the receiver to his left hand.

"I hope," the adjuster went on, "this is not because you hold against me anything I have done."

"No, it's nothing you've done," Davis said, and thought: it's what you are.

"What I did, I was trying to help."

"I know."

"I am inviting you to break bread, I am inviting you to a *banquet*, and all the time you are thinking: 'He made me lie, he made me go against my honor.' That is the way it has always been with you people. There you have the whole story. Listen, such pure people like you should not get into accidents." The adjuster went on and on; the complaint seemed old, a song, a chant, the truth of it not in the words but in the tone itself. Finally he stopped, and apologized, and Davis said that there was no need. He thanked the adjuster for his help and hung up.

On Sunday morning he went to the corner for a newspaper and when he came back he saw that the hood of his car was open. One boy was leaning over the engine and another was sitting in the front seat with the door open. The radio was on. "Hey, you kids," Davis yelled, and they looked up. The one under the hood was Richie. "I didn't know it was you," Davis said, coming up to them.

"I see you had it fixed," Richie said. "How much it put you back?"

Davis named a price three hundred dollars less than what he had paid, not wanting to look like a sucker. Apparently even this figure was not low enough. "Jeez," said the boy in the front seat, and rolled his eyes.

"What the hell." Richie closed the hood harder than was necessary. "As long as it wasn't your money."

Davis had the lock fixed but still he worried. There were quite a few souped-up cars in the neighborhood and he had to stop himself from going to the window when one of them started up outside or passed in the street. He heard them in his sleep. Often they entered his dreams. This went on for weeks after the car was stolen.

One night, in a prankish and suicidal mood, the thieves drove Davis's car up and down the street at a terrific speed. Davis stirred in recognition; his dream changed, delivered him to a flat and lonely stretch of road outside Shreveport. He was in the old car with his friend. A half-empty bottle rolled on the seat between them. His friend had the pedal pushed to the floor: the white line trembled like a blown thread between the lights, and the tall roadside pines ticked by like fenceposts. They were singing, heads thrown back and teeth bared.

The thieves were singing too. They turned at the end of the block and made another pass down the street. Outside Davis's window they shifted down, and the engine detonated. Davis bolted up from sleep, hand over breast, as if his own heart had misfired.

Wingfield

When we arrived at the camp they pulled us off the buses and made us do push-ups in the parking lot. The asphalt was hot and tar stuck to our noses. They made fun of our clothes and took them away from us. They shaved our heads until little white scars showed through, then filled our arms with boots and belts and helmets and punctured them with needles.

In the middle of the night they came to our barracks and walked up and down between us as we stood by our bunks. They looked at us. If we looked at them they said, "Why are you looking at me?" and made us do push-ups. If you didn't act right they made your life sad.

They divided us into companies, platoons, and squads. In my squad were Wingfield and Parker and seven others. Parker was a wise guy, my friend. I never saw anything get him down except malaria. Wingfield, before the military took responsibility for him, had been kept alive somewhere in North Carolina. When he was in a condition to talk his voice oozed out of him thick and slow and sweet. His eyes when he had them open were the palest blue. Most of the time they were closed.

He often fell asleep while he polished his boots, and once while he was shaving. They ordered him to paint baseboards and he curled up in the corner and let the baseboards take care of themselves. They found him with his head resting on his outstretched arm, his mouth open; a string of paint had dried between the brush and the floor.

In the afternoons they showed us films: from these we learned how to maintain our jeeps, how to protect our teeth from decay, how to treat foreigners, and how to sheathe ourselves against boils, nervous disorders, madness, and finally the long night of the blind. The foreigners wore shiny suits and carried briefcases. They smiled as they directed our soldiers to their destinations. They would do the same for us if we could remember how to ask them questions. As we repeated the important phrases to ourselves we could hear the air whistling in and out of Wingfield's mouth, rattling in the depths of his throat.

Wingfield slept as they showed us how our weapons worked, and what plants we could browse on if we got lost or ran out of food. Sometimes they caught him and made him stand up; he would smile shyly, like a young girl, and find something to lean against, and go back to sleep. He slept while we marched, which other soldiers could do; but other soldiers marched straight when they were supposed to turn and turned when they were supposed to march straight. They marched into trees and ditches and walls, they fell into holes. Wingfield could march around corners while asleep. He could sing the cadence and double-time at port arms without opening his eyes. You had to see it to believe it.

At the end of our training they drove us deep into the woods and set our company against another. To make the numbers even they gave the other side six of our men, Wingfield among them. He did not want to go but they made him. Then they handed out blank ammunition and colored scarves, blue for us and red for them.

The presence of these two colors made the woods dangerous. We tiptoed from bush to bush, crawled on our stomachs through brown needles under the stunted pines. The bark of the trees was sweating amber resin but you couldn't stop and stare. If you dawdled and daydreamed you would be taken in ambush. When soldiers with red scarves walked by we hid and shot them from behind and sent them to the parking lot, which was no longer a parking lot but the land of the dead.

A wind sprang up, bending and shaking the trees; their shadows lunged at us. Then darkness fell over the woods, sudden as a trap closing. Here and there we saw a stab of flame and heard a shot, but soon this scattered firing fell away. We pitched tents and posted guards; sat in silence and ate food from cans, cold. Our heartbeats echoed in our helmets.

Parker threw rocks. We heard them thumping the earth, breaking brittle branches as they fell. Someone yelled at him to stop, and Parker pointed where the shout came from.

Then we blackened our faces and taped our jingling dog tags, readied ourselves to raid. We slipped into the darkness as though we belonged there, like shadows. Gnats swarmed, mosquitos stung us but we did not slap; we were that stealthy. We went on until we saw, not far ahead, a fire. A fire! The fools had made a fire! Parker put his hand over his mouth and shook his head from side to side, signifying laughter. The rest of us did the same.

We only had to find the guards to take the camp by surprise. I found one right away, mumbling and exclaiming in his sleep, his rifle propped against a tree. It was Wingfield. With hatred and contempt and joy I took him from behind, and as I drew it across his throat I was wishing that my finger was a knife. Twisting in my arms, he looked into my black face and said, "Oh my God," as though I was no impostor but Death himself.

Then we stormed the camp, firing into the figures lumped in

sleeping bags, firing into the tents and into the shocked white faces at the tent flaps. It was exactly the same thing that happened to us a year and three months later as we slept beside a canal in the Mekong Delta, a few kilometers from Ben Tré.

We were sent home on leave when our training ended, and when we regrouped, several of us were missing, sick or AWOL or sent overseas to fill the ranks of units picked clean in the latest fighting. Wingfield was among them. I never saw him again and I never expected to. From now on his nights would be filled with shadows like me, and against such enemies what chance did Wingfield have?

Parker got malaria two weeks before the canal attack, and was still in the hospital when it happened. When he got out they sent him to another unit. He wrote letters to me but I never answered them. They were full of messages for people who weren't alive any more, and I thought it would be a good thing if he never knew this. Then he would lose only one friend instead of twenty-six. At last the letters stopped and I did not hear from him again for nine years, when he knocked on my door one evening just after I'd come home from work.

He had written my parents, he explained, and they had told him where I was living. He said that he and his wife and daughter were just passing through on their way to Canada, but I knew better. There were other ways to go than this and travelers always took them. He wanted an accounting.

Parker's daughter played with my dogs and his wife cooked steaks in the barbecue pit while we drank beer and talked and looked each other over. He was still cheerful, but in a softer, slower way, like a jovial uncle of the boy he'd been. After we ate we lay on the blanket until the bugs got to our ankles and the child began to whine. Parker's wife carried the dishes into the house and washed them while we settled on the steps. The light from the kitchen window laid a garish patch upon the lawn. Things crawled toward it under the grass. Parker asked the question he'd come to ask and then sat back and waited while I spoke name after name into the night. When I finished he said, "Is that all? What about Washington?"

"I told you. He got home all right."

"You're sure about that?"

"Of course I'm sure."

"You ought to get married," Parker said, standing up. "You take yourself too seriously. What the hell, right?"

Parker's daughter was lying on the living-room floor next to my golden retriever, who growled softly in his sleep as Parker lifted the girl and slung her over his shoulder. His wife took my arm and leaned against me as we walked out to the car. "I feel so comfortable with you," she said. "You remined me of my grandfather."

"By the way," Parker said, "do you remember Wingfield?"

"He was with that first bunch that got sent over," I said. "I don't think he made it back."

"Who told you that?"

"Nobody. I just don't think he did."

"You're wrong. I saw him." Parker shifted the girl to his other shoulder. "That's what I was going to tell you. I was in Charlotte six months ago and I saw him in the train station, sitting on a bench."

"You didn't."

"Oh yes I did."

"How was he? What did he say?"

"He didn't say anything. I was in a hurry and he looked so peaceful I just couldn't bring myself to wake him up."

"But it was definitely him?"

"It was Wingfield all right. He had his mouth open."

I waved at their car until it made the turn at the end of the street. Then I rummaged through the garbage and filled the dogs' bowls with the bones and gristle Parker's wife had thrown away. As I inspected the dishes she had washed the thought came to me that this was a fussy kind of thing for a young man to do.

I opened a bottle of wine and went outside. The coals in the cooking pit hissed and flushed as the wind played over them, pulling away the smoke in tight spirals. I sensed the wings of the bats above me, wheeling in the darkness. Like a soldier on leave, like a boy who knows nothing at all, like a careless and go-to-hell fellow I drank to them. Then I drank to the crickets and locusts and cicadas who purred so loudly that the earth itself seemed to be snoring. I drank to the snoring earth, to the closed eye of the moon, to the trees that nodded and sighed: until, already dreaming, I fell back upon the blanket.

In the Garden of the North
American Martyrs

When she was young, Mary saw a brilliant and original man lose his job because he had expressed ideas that were offensive to the trustees of the college where they both taught. She shared his views, but did not sign the protest petition. She was, after all, on trial herself—as a teacher, as a woman, as an interpreter of history.

Mary watched herself. Before giving a lecture she wrote it out in full, using the arguments and often the words of other, approved writers, so that she would not by chance say something scandalous. Her own thoughts she kept to herself, and the words for them grew faint as time went on; without quite disappearing they shrank to remote, nervous points, like birds flying away.

When the department turned into a hive of cliques, Mary went about her business and pretended not to know that people hated each other. To avoid seeming bland she let herself become eccentric in harmless ways. She took up bowling, which she learned to love, and founded the Brandon College chapter of a society dedicated to restoring the good name of Richard III. She memorized comedy routines from records and jokes from books; people groaned when she rattled them off, but she did not let that stop her, and after a time the groans became the point of the jokes. They were a kind of tribute to Mary's willingness to expose herself.

In fact no one at the college was safer than Mary, for she was making herself into something institutional, like a custom, or a mascot—part of the college's idea of itself.

Now and then she wondered whether she had been too careful. The things she said and wrote seemed flat to her, pulpy, as though someone else had squeezed the juice out of them. And once, while talking with a senior professor, Mary saw herself reflected in a window: she was leaning toward him and had her head turned so that her ear was right in front of his moving mouth. The sight disgusted her. Years later, when she had to get a hearing aid, Mary suspected that her deafness was a result of always trying to catch everything everyone said.

In the second half of Mary's fifteenth year at Brandon the provost called a meeting of all faculty and students to announce that the college was bankrupt and would not open its gates again. He was every bit as much surprised as they; the report from the trustees had reached his desk only that morning. It seemed that Brandon's financial manager had speculated in some kind of futures and lost everything. The provost wanted to deliver the news in person before it reached the papers. He wept openly and so did the students and teachers, with only a few exceptions—some cynical upperclassmen who claimed to despise the education they had received.

Mary could not rid her mind of the word "speculate." It meant to guess, in terms of money to gamble. How could a man gamble a college? Why would he want to do that, and how could it be that no one stopped him? To Mary, it seemed to belong to another time; she thought of a drunken plantation owner gaming away his slaves.

*   *   *

She applied for jobs and got an offer from a new experimental college in Oregon. It was her only offer so she took it.

The college was in one building. Bells rang all the time, lockers lined the hallways, and at every corner stood a buzzing water fountain. The student newspaper came out twice a month on mimeograph paper which felt wet. The library, which was next to the band room, had no librarian and no books.

The countryside was beautiful, though, and Mary might have enjoyed it if the rain had not caused her so much trouble. There was something wrong with her lungs that the doctors couldn't agree on, and couldn't cure; whatever it was, the dampness made it worse. On rainy days condensation formed in Mary's hearing aid and shorted it out. She began to dread talking with people, never knowing when she would have to take out her control box and slap it against her leg.

It rained nearly every day. When it was not raining it was getting ready to rain, or clearing. The ground glinted under the grass, and the light had a yellow undertone that flared up during storms.

There was water in Mary's basement. Her walls sweated, and she had found toadstools growing behind the refrigerator. She felt as though she were rusting out, like one of those old cars people thereabouts kept in their front yards, on pieces of wood. Mary knew that everyone was dying, but it did seem to her that she was dying faster than most.

She continued to look for another job, without success. Then, in the fall of her third year in Oregon, she got a letter from a woman named Louise who'd once taught at Brandon. Louise had scored a great success with a book on Benedict Arnold and was now on the faculty of a famous college in upstate New York. She said that one of her colleagues would be retiring at the end of the year and asked whether Mary would be interested in the position.

The letter surprised Mary. Louise thought of herself as a great historian and of almost everyone else as useless; Mary had not known that she felt differently about her. Moreover, enthusiasm for other people's causes did not come easily to Louise, who had a way of sucking in her breath when familiar names were mentioned, as though she knew things that friendship kept her from disclosing.

Mary expected nothing, but sent a résumé and copies of her two books. Shortly after that Louise called to say that the search committee, of which she was chairwoman, had decided to grant Mary an interview in early November. "Now don't get your hopes *too* high," Louise said.

"Oh, no," Mary said, but thought: Why shouldn't I hope? They would not go to the bother and expense of bringing her to the college if they weren't serious. And she was certain that the interview would go well. She would make them like her, or at least give them no cause to dislike her.

She read about the area with a strange sense of familiarity, as if the land and its history were already known to her. And when her plane left Portland and climbed easterly into the clouds, Mary felt like she was going home. The feeling stayed with her, growing stronger when they landed. She tried to describe it to Louise as they left the airport at Syracuse and drove toward the college, an hour or so away. "It's like *déjà vu*," she said.

"*Déjà vu* is a hoax," Louise said. "It's just a chemical imbalance of some kind."

"Maybe so," Mary said, "but I still have this sensation."

"Don't get serious on me," Louise said. "That's not your long suit. Just be your funny, wisecracking old self. Tell me now— honestly—how do I look?"

It was night, too dark to see Louise's face well, but in the airport she had seemed gaunt and pale and intense. She reminded Mary of a description in the book she'd been reading, of how Iroquois warriors gave themselves visions by fasting. She had that kind of look about her. But she wouldn't want to hear that. "You look wonderful," Mary said.

"There's a reason," Louise said. "I've taken a lover. My concentration has improved, my energy level is up, and I've lost ten pounds. I'm also getting some color in my cheeks, though that could be the weather. I recommend the experience highly. But you probably disapprove."

Mary didn't know what to say. She said that she was sure Louise knew best, but that didn't seem to be enough. "Marriage is a great institution," she added, "but who wants to live in an institution?"

Louise groaned. "I know you," she said, "and I know that right now you're thinking 'But what about Ted? What about the children?' The fact is, Mary, they aren't taking it well at all. Ted has become a nag." She handed Mary her purse. "Be a good girl and light me a cigarette, will you? I know I told you I quit, but this whole thing has been very hard on me, very hard, and I'm afraid I've started again."

They were in the hills now, heading north on a narrow road. Tall trees arched above them. As they topped a rise Mary saw the forest all around, deep black under the plum-colored sky. There were a few lights and these made the darkness seem even greater.

"Ted has succeeded in completely alienating the children from me," Louise was saying. "There is no reasoning with any of them. In fact, they refuse to discuss the matter at all, which is very ironical because over the years I have tried to instill in them a willingness to see things from the other person's point of view. If they could just *meet* Jonathan I know they would feel differently. But they won't hear of it. Jonathan," she said, "is my lover."

"I see," Mary said, and nodded.

Coming around a curve they caught two deer in the headlights. Their eyes lit up and their hindquarters tensed; Mary could see them trembling as the car went by. "Deer," she said.

"I don't know," Louise said, "I just don't know. I do my best and it never seems to be enough. But that's enough about me — let's talk about you. What did you think of my latest book?" She squawked and beat her palms on the steering wheel. "God, I love that joke," she said. "Seriously, though, what about you? It must have been a real shockeroo when good old Brandon folded."

"It was hard. Things haven't been good but they'll be a lot better if I get this job."

"At least you have work," Louise said. "You should look at it from the bright side."

"I try."

"You seem so gloomy. I hope you're not worrying about the interview, or the class. Worrying won't do you a bit of good. Be happy."

"Class? What class?"

"The class you're supposed to give tomorrow, after the interview. Didn't I tell you? *Mea culpa*, hon, *mea maxima culpa*. I've been uncharacteristically forgetful lately."

"But what will I do?"

"Relax," Louise said. "Just pick a subject and wing it."

"Wing it?"

"You know, open your mouth and see what comes out. Extemporize."

"But I always work from a prepared lecture."

Louise sighed. "All right. I'll tell you what. Last year I wrote an article on the Marshall Plan that I got bored with and never published. You can read that."

Parroting what Louise had written seemed wrong to Mary, at first; then it occurred to her that she had been doing the same kind of thing for many years, and that this was not the time to get scruples. "Thanks," she said. "I appreciate it."

"Here we are," Louise said, and pulled into a circular drive with several cabins grouped around it. In two of the cabins lights were on; smoke drifted straight up from the chimneys. "This is the visitors' center. The college is another two miles thataway." Louise pointed down the road. "I'd invite you to stay at my house, but I'm spending the night with Jonathan and Ted is not good company these days. You would hardly recognize him."

She took Mary's bags from the trunk and carried them up the steps of a darkened cabin. "Look," she said, "they've laid a fire for you. All you have to do is light it." She stood in the middle of the room with her arms crossed and watched as Mary held a match under the kindling. "There," she said. "You'll be snugaroo in no time. I'd love to stay and chew the fat but I can't. You just get a good night's sleep and I'll see you in the morning."

Mary stood in the doorway and waved as Louise pulled out of the drive, spraying gravel. She filled her lungs, to taste the air: it was tart and clear. She could see the stars in their figurations, and the vague streams of light that ran among the stars.

She still felt uneasy about reading Louise's work as her own. It would be her first complete act of plagiarism. It would change her. It would make her less—how much less, she did not know. But what else could she do? She certainly couldn't "wing it." Words might fail her, and then what? Mary had a dread of silence. When she thought of silence she thought of drowning, as if it were a kind of water she could not swim in.

"I want this job," she said, and settled deep into her coat. It was cashmere and Mary had not worn it since moving to Oregon, because people there thought you were pretentious if you had on anything but a Pendleton shirt or, of course, raingear. She rubbed her cheek against the upturned collar and thought of a silver moon shining through bare black branches, a white house with green shutters, red leaves falling in a hard blue sky.

Louise woke her a few hours later. She was sitting on the edge of the bed, pushing at Mary's shoulder and snuffling loudly. When Mary asked her what was wrong she said, "I want your opinion on something. It's very important. Do you think I'm womanly?"

Mary sat up. "Louise, can this wait?"

"No."

"Womanly?"

Louise nodded.

"You are very beautiful," Mary said, "and you know how to present yourself."

Louise stood and paced the room. "That son of a bitch," she said. She came back and stood over Mary. "Let's suppose someone said I have no sense of humor. Would you agree or disagree?"

"In some things you do. I mean, yes, you have a good sense of humor."

"What do you mean, 'in some things'? What kind of things?"

"Well, if you heard that someone had been killed in an unusual way, like by an exploding cigar, you would think that was funny."

Louise laughed.

"That's what I mean," Mary said.

Louise went on laughing. "Oh, Lordy," she said. "Now it's my turn to say something about you." She sat down beside Mary.

"Please," Mary said.

"Just one thing," Louise said.

Mary waited.

"You're trembling," Louise said. "I was just going to say—oh, forget it. Listen, do you mind if I sleep on the couch? I'm all in."

"Go ahead."

"Sure it's okay? You've got a big day tomorrow." She fell back on the sofa and kicked off her shoes. "I was just going to say, you should use some liner on those eyebrows of yours. They sort of disappear and the effect is disconcerting."

Neither of them slept. Louise chain-smoked cigarettes and Mary watched the coals burn down. When it was light enough that they could see each other Louise got up. "I'll send a student for you," she said. "Good luck."

The college looked the way colleges are supposed to look. Roger, the student assigned to show Mary around, explained that it was an exact copy of a college in England, right down to the gargoyles and stained-glass windows. It looked so much like a college that moviemakers sometimes used it as a set. *Andy Hardy Goes to Col-*

lege had been filmed there, and every fall they had an Andy Hardy Goes to College Day, with raccoon coats and goldfish-swallowing contests.

Above the door of the Founder's Building was a Latin motto which, roughly translated, meant "God helps those who help themselves." As Roger recited the names of illustrious graduates Mary was struck by the extent to which they had taken this precept to heart. They had helped themselves to railroads, mines, armies, states; to empires of finance with outposts all over the world.

Roger took Mary to the chapel and showed her a plaque bearing the names of alumni who had been killed in various wars, all the way back to the Civil War. There were not many names. Here too, apparently, the graduates had helped themselves. "Oh yes," Roger said as they were leaving, "I forgot to tell you. The communion rail comes from some church in Europe where Charlemagne used to go."

They went to the gymnasium, and the three hockey rinks, and the library, where Mary inspected the card catalogue, as though she would turn down the job if they didn't have the right books. "We have a little more time," Roger said as they went outside. "Would you like to see the power plant?"

Mary wanted to keep busy until the last minute, so she agreed.

Roger led her into the depths of the service building, explaining things about the machine, which was the most advanced in the country. "People think the college is really old-fashioned," he said, "but it isn't. They let girls come here now, and some of the teachers are women. In fact, there's a statute that says they have to interview at least one woman for each opening. There it is."

They were standing on an iron catwalk above the biggest machine Mary had ever beheld. Roger, who was majoring in Earth Sciences, said that it had been built from a design pioneered by a professor in his department. Where before he had been gabby Roger now became reverent. It was clear that for him this machine was the soul of the college, that the purpose of the college was to provide outlets for the machine. Together they leaned against the railing and watched it hum.

Mary arrived at the committee room exactly on time for her interview, but the room was empty. Her two books were on the table, along with a water pitcher and some glasses. She sat down and picked up one of the books. The binding cracked as she opened it. The pages were smooth, clean, unread. Mary turned to the first chapter, which began, "It is generally believed that . . ." How dull, she thought.

Nearly twenty minutes later Louise came in with several men. "Sorry we're late," she said. "We don't have much time so we'd better get started." She introduced Mary to the men, but with one exception the names and faces did not stay together. The exception was Dr. Howells, the department chairman, who had a porous blue nose and terrible teeth.

A shiny-faced man to Dr. Howells's right spoke first. "So," he said, "I understand you once taught at Brandon College."

"It was a shame that Brandon had to close," said a young man with a pipe in his mouth. "There is a place for schools like Brandon." As he talked the pipe wagged up and down.

"Now you're in Oregon," Dr. Howells said. "I've never been there. How do you like it?"

"Not very much," Mary said.

"Is that right?" Dr. Howells leaned toward her. "I thought everyone liked Oregon. I hear it's very green."

"That's true," Mary said.

"I suppose it rains a lot," he said.

"Nearly every day."

"I wouldn't like that," he said, shaking his head. "I like it dry. Of course it snows here, and you have your rain now and then, but it's a *dry* rain. Have you ever been to Utah? There's a state for you. Bryce Canyon. The Mormon Tabernacle Choir."

"Dr. Howells was brought up in Utah," said the young man with the pipe.

"It was a different place altogether in those days," Dr. Howells said. "Mrs. Howells and I have always talked about going back when I retire, but now I'm not so sure."

"We're a little short on time," Louise said.

"And here I've been going on and on," Dr. Howells said. "Before we wind things up, is there anything you want to tell us?"

"Yes. I think you should give me the job." Mary laughed when she said this, but no one laughed back, or even looked at her. They all looked away. Mary understood then that they were not really considering her for the position. She had been brought here to satisfy a rule. She had no hope.

The men gathered their papers and shook hands with Mary and told her how much they were looking forward to her class. "I can't get enough of the Marshall Plan," Dr. Howells said.

"Sorry about that," Louise said when they were alone. "I didn't think it would be so bad. That was a real bitcheroo."

"Tell me something," Mary said. "You already know who you're going to hire, don't you?"

Louise nodded.

"Then why did you bring me here?"

Louise began to explain about the statute and Mary interrupted. "I know all that. But why me? Why did you pick *me*?"

Louise walked to the window. She spoke with her back to Mary. "Things haven't been going very well for old Louise," she said. "I've been unhappy and I thought you might cheer me up. You used to be so funny, and I was sure you would enjoy the trip—it didn't cost you anything, and it's pretty this time of year with the leaves and everything. Mary, you don't know the things my parents did to me. And Ted is no barrel of laughs either. Or Jonathan, the son of a bitch. I deserve some love and friendship but I don't get any." She turned and looked at her watch. "It's almost time for your class. We'd better go."

"I would rather not give it. After all, there's not much point, is there?"

"But you *have* to give it. That's part of the interview." Louise handed Mary a folder. "All you have to do is read this. It isn't much, considering all the money we've laid out to get you here."

Mary followed Louise down the hall to the lecture room. The professors were sitting in the front row with their legs crossed. They smiled and nodded at Mary. Behind them the room was full of students, some of whom had spilled over into the aisles. One of the professors adjusted the microphone to Mary's height, crouching down as he went to the podium and back as though he would prefer not to be seen.

Louise called the room to order. She introduced Mary and gave the subject of the lecture. But Mary had decided to wing it after all. Mary came to the podium unsure of what she would say; sure only that she would rather die than read Louise's article. The sun poured through the stained glass onto the people around her, painting their faces. Thick streams of smoke from the young professor's pipe drifted through a circle of red light at Mary's feet, turning crimson and twisting like flames.

"I wonder how many of you know," she began, "that we are in the Long House, the ancient domain of the Five Nations of the Iroquois."

Two professors looked at each other.

"The Iroquois were without pity," Mary said. "They hunted people down with clubs and arrows and spears and nets, and blowguns made from elder stalks. They tortured their captives, sparing no one, not even the little children. They took scalps and practiced cannibalism and slavery. Because they had no pity they became powerful, so powerful that no other tribe dared to oppose them. They made the other tribes pay tribute, and when they had nothing more to pay the Iroquois attacked them."

Several of the professors began to whisper. Dr. Howells was saying something to Louise, and Louise was shaking her head.

"In one of their raids," Mary said, "they captured two Jesuit priests, Jean de Brébeuf and Gabriel Lalement. They covered Lalement with pitch and set him on fire in front of Brébeuf. When Brébeuf rebuked them they cut off his lips and put a burning iron down his throat. They hung a collar of red-hot hatchets around his neck, and poured boiling water over his head. When he continued to preach to them they cut strips of flesh from his body and ate them before his eyes. While he was still alive they scalped him and cut open his breast and drank his blood. Later, their chief tore out Brébeuf's heart and ate it, but just before he did this Brébeuf spoke to them one last time. He said—"

"That's enough!" yelled Dr. Howells, jumping to his feet.

Louise stopped shaking her head. Her eyes were perfectly round.

Mary had come to the end of her facts. She did not know what Brébeuf had said. Silence rose up around her; just when she thought she would go under and be lost in it she heard someone whistling in the hallway outside, trilling the notes like a bird, like many birds.

"Mend your lives," she said. "You have deceived yourselves in the pride of your hearts, and the strength of your arms. Though you soar aloft like the eagle, though your nest is set among the stars, thence I will bring you down, says the Lord. Turn from power to love. Be kind. Do justice. Walk humbly."

Louise was waving her arms. "Mary!" she shouted.

But Mary had more to say, much more; she waved back at Louise, then turned off her hearing aid so that she would not be distracted again.

Poaching

Wharton was a cartoonist, and a nervous man — "high-strung," he would have said. Because of his occupation and his nerves he required peace, but in Vancouver he didn't get much of that. His wife, Ellen, was deficient in many respects, and resented his constructive criticism. She took it personally. They bickered, and she threatened to leave him. Wharton believed that she was having an affair. George, their son, slouched around the house all day and paid no attention when Wharton described all the sports and hobbies that an eleven-year-old boy ought to be interested in.

Wharton dreamed of a place in the country where George would be outside all day, making friends and hiking, and Ellen would have a garden. In his dream Wharton saw her look up and smile as he came toward her.

He sometimes went camping for a few days when things got bad at home. On one of these trips he saw a large piece of land that the government was selling and decided to buy it. The property was heavily wooded, had a small pond surrounded by birch trees, and a good sturdy building. The building needed some work, but Wharton thought that such a project would bring them all together.

When he told Ellen about it she said, "Are you kidding?"

"I've never been more serious," Wharton said. "And it wouldn't hurt you to show a little enthusiasm."

"No way," Ellen said. "Count me out."

Wharton went ahead and arranged the move. He was sure that when the moment came, Ellen would go with them. He never lost this conviction, not even when she got a job and had a lawyer draw up separation papers. But the moment came and went, and finally Wharton and George left without her.

They had been on the land for almost a year when Wharton began to hear shots from beyond the meadow. The shooting woke him at dawn and disturbed him at his work, and he couldn't make up his mind what to do. He hoped that it would just stop. The noise had begun to wake George, and in his obsessive way he would not leave off asking questions about it. Also, though he seldom played there, George had developed a sense of injury at being kept out of the woods. Ellen was coming up for a visit—her first—and she would make a stink.

The shooting continued. It went on for two weeks, three weeks, well past Easter. On the morning of the day Ellen was supposed to arrive Wharton heard two shots, and he knew he had to do something. He decided to go and talk to his neighbor Vernon. Vernon understood these things.

George caught Wharton leaving the house and asked if he could go play with his friend Rory.

"Absolutely not," Wharton said, and headed up the path toward the road. The ground was swollen and spongy with rain. The fenceposts had a black and soggy look, and the ditches on either side of the road were loud with the rushing of water. Wharton dodged mudholes, huffing a little, and contemplated Rory.

To help George make friends during the previous summer

Wharton had driven him to a quarry where the local children swam. George splashed around by himself at one end and pretended that he was having a fine old time, as his eyes ticked back and forth to the motion of the other children flying from bank to bank on the rope swing, shouting "Banzai!" when they let go and reached out to the water.

One afternoon Wharton built a fire and produced hot dogs for the children to roast. He asked their names and introduced George. He told them that they should feel free to come and visit George whenever they liked. They could swim in the pond, or play hide-and-seek in the woods. When they had eaten they thanked him and went back to their end of the quarry while George went back to his. Wharton considered rounding them up for a nature walk, but he never got around to it. A few days before the weather turned too cold for swimming George caught a garter snake in the rushes by the bank, and another boy came over to take a look. That night George asked if he could sleep over at Rory's.

"Who's Rory?"

"Just a guy."

Rory eventually came to their house for a reciprocal visit. Wharton did not think that he was an acceptable friend for George. He would not meet Wharton's eye, and had a way of laughing to himself. Rory and George whispered and giggled all night, and a few days later Wharton found several burnt matches in George's room which George would not account for. He hoped that the boy would enlarge his circle of friends when school began, but this never happened. Wharton fretted about George's shyness. Friends were a blessing and he wanted George to have many friends. In Wharton's opinion, George's timidity was the result of his being underdeveloped physically. Wharton advised him to take up weight lifting.

Over the mountains to the east a thin line of clouds was getting thicker. Wharton felt a growing dampness in the air as he turned into his neighbor's gate.

He disliked having to ask Vernon for favors or advice, but at times he had no choice. Twice during the winter his car had slipped off the icy, unbanked road, and both times Vernon had pulled him out. He showed Wharton how to keep the raccoons out of his garbage, and how to use a chain saw. Wharton was grateful, but he suspected that Vernon had begun to think of himself as his superior.

He found Vernon in the yard, loading five-gallon cans into the back of his truck. This pleased Wharton. He would not have to go into the dirty, evil-smelling house. Vernon had rented most of the place out to a commune from Seattle, and Wharton was appalled at their sloth and resolute good cheer. He was further relieved not to have to go inside, because he wished to avoid one of the women. They had kept company for a short, unhappy time during the winter; the situation was complicated, and Wharton already had enough to keep him busy for the day.

"Well howdy there," Vernon said. "And how's every little thing down at the lower forty?"

Wharton noticed that Vernon always countrified his speech when he was around. He guessed that Vernon did it to make him feel like a city slicker. Wharton had heard him talk to other people and he sounded normal enough. "Not so good," he said, and lifted one of the cans.

Vernon took it from him very firmly and slid it down the bed of the truck. "You got to use your back hoisting these things," he said. He slammed the tailgate shut and yanked the chain through the slots. The links rattled like bolts in a can. He took a rag out of his back pocket and blew his nose. "What's the trouble?"

"Someone's been shooting on my land."

"What do you mean, shooting? Shooting what?"

"I don't know. Deer, I suppose."

Vernon shook his head. "Deer have all headed back into the high country by now."

"Well, whatever. Squirrels. Rabbits. The point is that someone has been hunting in the woods without asking my permission."

"It isn't any of us," Vernon said. "I can tell you that much. There's only one rifle in this house and nobody goes near it but me. I wouldn't trust that load of fruitcakes with an empty water pistol."

"I didn't think it was you. It just occurred to me that you might have some idea who it could be. You know the people around here."

Vernon creased his brow and narrowed his eyes to show, Wharton supposed, that he was thinking. "There's one person," he said finally. "You know Jeff Gill from up the road?"

Wharton shook his head.

"I guess you wouldn't have met him at that. He keeps to himself. He's pretty crazy, Jeff Gill. You know that song 'I'm My Own Grandpaw'? Well, Jeff Gill is his own uncle. The Gills," he said, "are a right close family. You want me to call down there, see what's going on?"

"I would appreciate that."

Wharton waited outside, leaning against an empty watering trough. The breeze rippled puddles and blew scraps of paper across the yard. Somewhere a door creaked open and shut. He tried to count the antlers on the front of the barn but gave up. There were over a hundred pairs of them, bleached and silvered by the sun. It was a wonder there were any deer left in the province. Over the front door of the house there were more antlers, and on the porch a set of suitcases and a steamer trunk. Apparently someone was leaving the commune. If so, it would not be the first defection.

Vernon's tenants had had a pretty awful winter. Factions developed over the issues of child care and discipline, sleeping arrangements, cooking, shoveling snow, and the careless use of someone's Deutschegrammophon records. According to Wharton's lady friend, Vernon had caused a lot of trouble. He made fun of the ideals of the commune with respect to politics, agriculture, religion, and diet, and would not keep his hands off the women. It got to where they were afraid to go out to the woodshed by themselves. Also, he insisted on calling them Hare Krishnas, which they were not.

Wharton's friend wanted to know why, if Vernon couldn't be more supportive of the commune, he had rented the house to them in the first place? And if he hated them so much how come he stayed on in the master bedroom?

Wharton knew the answer to the first question and could guess the answer to the second. Vernon's father had been a wild man and died owing twelve years' back taxes. Vernon needed money. Wharton imagined that he stayed on himself because he had grown up in the house and could not imagine living anywhere else.

Vernon came back into the yard carrying a rifle. Wharton could smell the oil from ten feet away. "I couldn't get anybody down at the Gills'," Vernon said. "Phone's been disconnected. I talked to a guy I knew who works with Jeff, and he says Jeff hasn't been at the mill in over a month. Thinks he's went somewhere else." Vernon held out the rifle. "You know how to work this?"

"Yes," Wharton said.

"Why don't you keep it around for awhile. Just till things get sorted out."

Wharton did not want the rifle. As he had told George when George asked for a B-B gun, he believed that firearms were a sign of weakness. He reached out and took the thing, but only because Vernon would feel slighted if he refused it.

"Wow," George said when he saw the rifle. "Are you going to shoot the sniper?"

"I'm not going to shoot anybody," Wharton said. "And I've told you before, the word is poacher, not sniper."

"Yeah, poacher. Where did you get the gun?"

Wharton looked down at his son. The boy had been sawing up and nailing together some scrap lumber. He was sweating and his skin had a flush on it. How thin he was! You would think he never fed the boy, when in fact he went out of his way to prepare wholesome meals for him. Wharton had no idea where the food went, unless, as he suspected, George was giving his lunches to Rory. Wharton began to describe to George the difference between a rifle and a gun but George was not interested. He would be perfectly content to use his present vocabulary for the next eighty years.

"When I was your age," he said, "I enjoyed acquiring new words and learning to use them correctly."

"I know, I know," George said, then mumbled something under his breath.

"What was that?"

"Nothing."

"You said something. Now what did you say?"

George sighed. "'Jeez.'"

Wharton was going to point out that if George wished to curse he should do so forthrightly, manfully, but he stopped himself. George was not a man, he was a boy, and boys should not be hounded all the time. They should be encouraged. Wharton nodded at the tangle of lumber and congratulated George on doing something both physical and creative. "What is it?" he asked.

"A lair," George said. "For a wolf."

"I see," Wharton said. "That's good." He nodded again and went inside. As he locked the rifle away—he didn't really know how to work it—Wharton decided that he should let George see his lighter side more often. He was capable of better conversation than reminders that "okay" was not a word, that it was prudent not to spend all one's allowance the same day, or that chairs were for sitting in and floors for walking on. Just the other day the plumber had come in to unclog the kitchen sink and he had laughed at several things Wharton had said.

For the rest of the morning Wharton sketched out episodes for his old bread-and-butter strip. This was about a trapper named Pierre who, in the course of his adventures, passed along bits of homespun philosophy and wilderness lore, such as how to treat frostbite and corns, and how to take bearings so that you would not end up walking in circles. The philosophy was anti-materialist, free-thinking stuff, much like the philosophy of Wharton's father, and over the years it had become obnoxious to him. He was mortally tired of the Trapper and his whole bag of tricks, his smugness and sermonizing and his endless cries of "Mon Dieu!" and "Sacre Bleu!" and "Ze ice, she ees breaking up!" Wharton was more interested in his new strip, *Ulysses*, whose hero was a dog searching for his master in the goldfields of the Yukon. Pierre still paid the bills, though, and Wharton could not afford to pull the plug on him.

There was no shooting from the woods, and Wharton's concentration ran deep. He worked in a reverie, and when he happened to look at his watch he realized that he was supposed to have picked up his wife ten minutes earlier. The station was an hour away.

Ellen kept after Wharton all the way home in her flat, smoky voice. She had old grievances and she listed them, but without anger, as if they bored her: his nagging, his slovenliness, his neglect of her. Oh, she didn't mind waiting around bus stations for an hour now and then. But he *always* kept her waiting. Why? Did he want to humiliate her? Was that it?

"No," Wharton said. "I just lost track of the time." The other charges she had brought against him were true and he did not challenge them.

"If there's one thing I can't stand," Ellen said, "it's this suffering-in-silence, stiff-upper-lip crap."

"I'm sorry," Wharton said.

"I know you are. That doesn't change anything. Oh, look at the little colts and fillies!"

Wharton glanced out the window. "Actually," he said, "those are ponies. Shetlands."

She didn't answer.

It rained hard, then cleared just before they came up the drive to the house. Ellen got out of the car and looked around skeptically. In the distance the mountains were draped with thick coils of cloud, and closer up in the foothills the mist lay among the treetops. Water ran down the trunks of the trees and stood everywhere. Wharton picked up Ellen's bags and walked toward the house, naming wildflowers along the path.

"I don't know what you're trying to prove," Ellen said, "living out in the middle of no goddam where at all." She saw George and shouted and waved. He dropped the board he was hammering and ran to meet her. She knelt on the wet grass and hugged him, pinning his arms to his side. He tried to hug back but finally gave up and waited, looking over Ellen's shoulder at Wharton. Wharton picked up his bags again. "I'll be in the house," he said, and continued up the path, his boots making a sucking noise in the mud.

"House?" Ellen said when she had come inside. "You call this a house? It's a barn or something."

"Actually," Wharton said, "it's a converted stable. The government used to keep mules here."

"I'm all for simple living but God Almighty."

"It's not so bad. We're getting along just fine, aren't we, George?"

"I guess so."

"Why don't you show Mother your room?"

"Okay." George went down the passageway. He waited outside,

holding the door like an usher. Ellen looked inside and nodded. "Oh, you set up a cot for me. Thank you, George."

"Dad set it up. I'll sleep there and you can have the bed if you want."

Wharton showed her what was left to see of the house. She hated it. "You don't even have any pictures on the walls!" she said. He admitted that the place lacked warm touches. In the summer he would throw on a coat of paint, maybe buy some curtains. When they came down from the loft where Wharton worked Ellen took a package from her suitcase and gave it to George.

"Well, George," Wharton said, "what do you say?"

"Thank you," George said, not to Ellen but to Wharton.

"Go ahead and open it," Wharton said.

"For Christ's sake," Ellen said.

It was a book, *The World of Wolves.* "Jeez," George said. He sat down on the floor and began thumbing through the pictures.

How could Ellen have guessed at George's interest in wolves? She had an instinct for gifts the way other people had an instinct for finding the right words to say. The world of things was not alien and distasteful to her as it was to Wharton. He despised his possessions with some ostentation; those who gave him gifts went away feeling as if they'd made Wharton party to a crime. He knew that over the years he had caused Ellen to be shy of her own generosity.

"Why don't you read in your bedroom, George? The light here is terrible."

"He can stay," Ellen said.

"Okay," George said, and went down the hall, not lifting his eyes from the page.

"That wasn't as expensive as it looks," Ellen said.

"It was a fine gift," Wharton said. "Wolves are one of George's obsessions these days."

"I got it for a song," Ellen said. She put a cigarette in her mouth and began to rummage through her purse. Finally she turned her bag upside down and dumped it all over the floor. She poked through the contents, then looked up. "Have you got a match?"

"No. You'll have to light it from the stove."

"I suppose you've quit." She said this as though it were an accusation.

"I still enjoy one every now and then," Wharton said.

"Did you read what that doctor said who did the post-mortem on Howard Hughes?" asked Ellen, returning from the kitchen. "He said, 'Howard Hughes had lungs just like a baby.' I almost cried when I read that, it made me so nostalgic for when I was young. I'd hate to think what my lungs look like, not to mention my liver and God knows what else." She blew out some smoke and watched it bitterly as it twisted through a slant of light.

"Howard Hughes never let anyone touch him or come close to him," Wharton said. "That's not your style."

"What do you mean by that?"

"Only that there's always a certain risk when we get close—"

"You didn't mean that. You think I've got this big love life going. What a laugh."

"Well, you did."

"I don't want to get into that," Ellen said. "Let's just say I like to be appreciated."

"I appreciated you."

"No. You thought you were too good for me."

Wharton denied this without heat. During most of their marriage he *had* imagined that he was too good for Ellen. He had been wrong about that and now look at the mess he had made. He stood abruptly, but once he was on his feet he could not think of anything to do, so he sat again.

"What's the point, anyway?" Ellen asked, waving her hand around. "Living in a stable, for God's sake, wearing those boots and that dumb hat."

"I was wearing the boots because the ground is muddy and the hat because my head gets cold."

"Who are you trying to kid? You wear the hat because you think it makes you look like Pierre the Trapper. Ees true, no?"

"You've made your point, Ellen. You don't like the house and you don't like me. Actually, I'm not even sure why you came."

"Actually," she said, "I came to see my son."

"I don't understand why you couldn't wait until June. That's only two more months and you'll have him all summer. According to the terms—"

Ellen snorted. "According to the terms," she said. "Come off it."

"Let me finish. I don't have to grant you visiting privileges. This is a courtesy visit. Now if you can't stop finding fault with everything you can leave, and the sooner the better."

"I'll leave tomorrow," Ellen said.

"Suit yourself."

Ellen bent suddenly in her chair. Piece by piece, she picked up the things she'd emptied onto the floor and replaced them in her purse. Then she stood and walked down the passageway to George's room, moving with dignity as if concealing drunkenness, or a limp.

At dinner George announced his intention to acquire a pet wolf. Wharton had entertained a similar fancy at George's age, and the smile he gave his son was addressed to the folly of both their imaginations. George took it as encouragement and pressed on. There was, he said, a man in Sinclair who had two breeding pairs of timber wolves. George knew for sure that a litter was expected any day now.

Wharton wanted to let George down lightly. "They're probably not real wolves," he said. "More likely they're German shepherds, or huskies, or a mix."

"These are real wolves all right," George said.

"How can you be sure?" Ellen asked. "Have you seen them?"

"No, but Rory has."

"Who is Rory?"

"Rory is an acquaintance of George's," Wharton said, "and Rory does not have the last word on every subject, at least not in this house."

"Rory is my friend," George said.

"All right," Wharton said, "I'm willing to accept Rory's testimony that those are real wolves. What I will not accept is the idea of bringing a wild animal into the house."

"They're not wild. Rory says—"

"Rory again!"

"—Rory says that they're just as tame as dogs, only smarter."

"George, be reasonable. A wolf is a killing machine. It needs to kill in order to survive. There's nothing wrong with that, but a wolf belongs in the wild, not on a chain or locked up in a cage somewhere."

"I wouldn't lock him up. He'd have a lair."

"A lair? Is that what you're building?"

George nodded. "I told you."

"George," Ellen said, "why don't you think about a nice dog? Wolves really are very dangerous animals."

George did not want a nice dog. He was willing to admit that wolves were dangerous, but only to the enemies of their friends. This carried him to his last argument, which he played like a trump: a wolf was just exactly what they needed to help them get rid of the sniper.

"Sniper?" Ellen said. "What sniper?"

"He means poacher," Wharton said. "George, I'm at the end of my patience. A wolf belongs with other wolves, not with people. I don't approve of this habit of turning wild animals into pets. Now please drop the subject. And stop playing with your food."

"What poacher?" Ellen asked.

"I'm not hungry," George said.

"Then leave the table."

George went to his room and slammed the door.

"What poacher?"

"Someone has been doing some shooting on the property. It's nothing serious."

"There's someone running around out there with a gun and you say it isn't serious?"

"This used to be public land. I want people to feel like they can use it."

"But this is your home!"

"Ellen—"

"What have you done about it? You haven't done anything at all, have you?"

"No," Wharton said, and got up and left the room. On his way outside he stopped to talk to George. The boy was sitting on the floor, sorting through some junk he kept in a cigar box. "Son," Wharton said, "I'm sorry if I was short with you at dinner."

"It's okay," George said.

"I'm not just being mean," Wharton said. "A mature wolf can weigh over a hundred and fifty pounds. Think what would happen if it turned on you."

"He wouldn't turn on me. He would protect me." George shook the box. "He would love me."

Wharton had intended to go for a walk but decided it was too slippery underfoot. He sat on the front steps instead, hunched down in his coat. The moon was racing through filmy clouds, melting at the edges. The wind had picked up considerably, and Wharton could hear trees creaking in the woods beyond. Gradually the sky lowered and it began to rain. Ellen came out and told Wharton that he had a phone call.

It was the woman from the commune. She was going to be leaving the next day and wanted to come up to say good-bye. Wharton told her that this was not possible just now. The woman was obviously hurt. She had once accused Wharton of not valuing her as a person and he wanted to show that this was not true. "Look," he said, "let me take you to the station tomorrow."

"Forget it."

Wharton insisted and finally she agreed. Only after he hung up did Wharton realize that he might have Ellen along as well. There was just one bus out on Sunday.

Ellen and George were lying on the floor, reading the book together. Ellen patted the place beside her. "Join us?" Wharton shook his head. They were getting on fine without him; he had no wish to break up such a cozy picture. Anyway it would hardly be appropriate for him to go flopping all over the floor after scolding George for the same thing. Still restless, he went up to the loft and worked. It was very late when he finished. He took off his boots at the foot of the ladder and moved as quietly as he could past George's bedroom. When he turned on the light in his own room he saw that Ellen was in his bed. She covered her eyes with her forearm. The soft flesh at the base of her throat fluttered gently with her breathing.

"Did you really want me to stay with George?"

"No," Wharton said. He dropped his clothes on top of the chest that served as dresser and chair. Ellen drew the covers back for him and he slid in beside her.

"Who was that on the phone?" she asked. "Have you got a little something going?"

"We saw each other a few times. The lady is leaving tomorrow."

"I'm sorry. I hate to think of you all alone out here."

Wharton almost said, "Then stay!" but he caught himself.

"There's something I've got to tell you," Ellen said, raising herself on an elbow. "Jesus, what a look."

"What have you got to tell me?"

"It isn't what you're thinking."

"You don't know what I'm thinking."

"The hell I don't." She sank back onto her side. "I'm leaving Vancouver," she said. "I'm not going to be able to take George this summer. That's why I wanted to see him now."

Ellen explained that she did not feel comfortable living alone in the city. She hated her job and the apartment was too small. She was going back to Victoria to see if she couldn't find something better there. She hated to let George down, but this was a bad time for her.

"Victoria? Why Victoria?" Ellen had never spoken well of the place. According to her the people were all stuffed shirts and there was nothing to do there. Wharton could not understand her and said so.

"Right now I need to be someplace I feel at home." That brought Ellen to another point. She was going to need money for travel and to keep body and soul together until she found another job.

"Whatever I can do," Wharton said.

"I knew you'd help."

"I guess this means you don't have to go back tomorrow."

"No. I guess not."

"Why don't you stay for a week? It would mean a lot to George."

"We'll see."

Wharton turned off the light, but he could not sleep for the longest time. Neither could Ellen; she kept turning and arranging herself. Wharton wanted to reach out to her but he wouldn't have felt right about it, so soon after lending her money.

George woke them in the morning. He sat on the edge of the bed, pale and trembling.

"What's wrong, sweetie?" Ellen asked, and then they heard a shot from the woods. She looked at Wharton. Wharton got out of bed, dressed quickly, and went outside.

He knew it was Jeff Gill, had known so the moment he heard the man's name. It sounded familiar, as things to come often did. He even knew what Jeff Gill would look like: short and wiry, with yellow teeth and close-set, porcine eyes. He did not know why Jeff Gill hated him but he surely did, and Wharton felt that in some way the hatred was justified.

It was raining, not hard but drearily. The air had a chill on it and as he circled the house Wharton walked into the mist of his own breathing. Two swallows skimmed the meadow behind the house, dipping and wheeling through the high grass. They did not break their pattern as he walked by them, yellow rubber boots glistening, and passed into the shadow of the tall trees.

He realized that he had not been in these woods for almost a month. He had been afraid to walk in his own land. He still was. "Go away!" he shouted, walking among the straight wet trunks of trees: "Go away!"

There were still clumps of snow lying everywhere, gray and crystalline and impacted with brown needles. The branches of pine and fir and spruce were tipped with sweet new growth. Stirred by the rain, the soil gave off an acid smell, like a compost heap. Wharton stepped under a sugar pine to catch his breath and scrape some of the mud off his boots. They were so heavy he could hardly lift them.

He heard another shot; it came from the direction of the pond and seemed to crash beside him. "Listen!" Wharton yelled. "I've got a rifle too and I'll use it! Go away!" Wharton thought that he was capable of doing what he said, if he had brought the weapon and had known how to work it. He had felt foolish and afraid for so long that he was becoming dangerous.

He walked toward the pond. The banks were ringed with silver birches and he leaned against one of these. The brown water bristled with splashing raindrops. He caught a motion on the surface of the pond, a rippling triangle like an arrowhead with a dark spot at its point. Wharton assumed that it was a duck and stepped out on a small jetty to get a better look.

Suddenly the creature raised its head and stared at Wharton. It was a beaver, swimming on its back. Its gaze was level and un-blinking. Its short front legs were folded over its gently rounded belly, reminding Wharton of a Hogarth engraving of an English clubman after a meal. The beaver lowered its head into the pond and then its belly disappeared and its paddle-like tail swung in a wide arc and cracked flat against the surface of the water. The birches around the pond squeezed the sound and made it sharp and loud, like a rifle going off.

Wharton turned and went back to the house and explained everything to Ellen and George. He made breakfast while they dressed, and afterwards they all walked down to the pond to look at the beaver. Along the way Wharton slipped and fell and when he tried to stand he fell again. The mud was on his face and even in his hair. Ellen told him that he ought to take a roll in the mud every day, that it would be the making of him.

George reached the bank first and shouted, "I see him! I see him!"

The beaver was old and out of place. A younger beaver had driven him away from his lodge, and during the thaw he had followed a seasonal stream, now gone dry, up to the pond.

When Vernon heard about the beaver he took his rifle back and went to the pond and shot him. Wharton was outraged, but Vernon insisted that the animal would have destroyed the birches and fouled the bottom of the pond, killing the plants and turning the water stagnant. George's biology teacher agreed.

Ellen left at the end of the week. She and Wharton wrote letters, and sometimes, late at night, she called him. They had good talks but they never lived together again. A few days after she left, George's friend Rory turned on him and threw his books and one of his shoes out the schoolbus window, with the help of another boy more to his liking.

But Wharton, standing in the warm rain with his family that morning, did not know that these things would come to pass. Nor did he know that the dog Ulysses would someday free him from the odious Trapper Pierre, or that George would soon—too soon—put on muscle and learn to take care of himself. The wind raised small waves and sent them slapping up against the jetty, so that it appeared to be sliding forward like the hull of a boat. Out in the pond the beaver dove and surfaced again. It seemed to Wharton, watching him move in wide circles upon the water, that the creature had been sent to them, that they had been offered an olive branch and were not far from home.

The Liar

My mother read everything except books. Advertisements on buses, entire menus as we ate, billboards; if it had no cover it interested her. So when she found a letter in my drawer that was not addressed to her she read it. "What difference does it make if James has nothing to hide?"—that was her thought. She stuffed the letter in the drawer when she finished it and walked from room to room in the big empty house, talking to herself. She took the letter out and read it again to get the facts straight. Then, without putting on her coat or locking the door, she went down the steps and headed for the church at the end of the street. No matter how angry and confused she might be, she always went to four o'clock Mass and now it was four o'clock.

It was a fine day, blue and cold and still, but Mother walked as though into a strong wind, bent forward at the waist with her feet hurrying behind in short, busy steps. My brother and sisters and I considered this walk of hers funny and we smirked at one another when she crossed in front of us to stir the fire, or water a plant. We didn't let her catch us at it. It would have puzzled her

153

to think that there might be anything amusing about her. Her one concession to the fact of humor was an insincere, startling laugh. Strangers often stared at her.

While Mother waited for the priest, who was late, she prayed. She prayed in a familiar, orderly, firm way: first for her late husband, my father, then for her parents—also dead. She said a quick prayer for my father's parents (just touching base; she had disliked them) and finally for her children in order of their ages, ending with me. Mother did not consider originality a virtue and until my name came up her prayers were exactly the same as on any other day.

But when she came to me she spoke up boldly. "I thought he wasn't going to do it any more. Murphy said he was cured. What am I supposed to do now?" There was reproach in her tone. Mother put great hope in her notion that I was cured. She regarded my cure as an answer to her prayers and by way of thanksgiving sent a lot of money to the Thomasite Indian Mission, money she had been saving for a trip to Rome. She felt cheated and she let her feelings be known. When the priest came in Mother slid back on the seat and followed the Mass with concentration. After communion she began to worry again and went straight home without stopping to talk to Frances, the woman who always cornered Mother after Mass to tell about the awful things done to her by Communists, devil-worshipers, and Rosicrucians. Frances watched her go with narrowed eyes.

Once in the house, Mother took the letter from my drawer and brought it into the kitchen. She held it over the stove with her fingernails, looking away so that she would not be drawn into it again, and set it on fire. When it began to burn her fingers she dropped it in the sink and watched it blacken and flutter and close upon itself like a fist. Then she washed it down the drain and called Dr. Murphy.

*   *   *

The letter was to my friend Ralphy in Arizona. He used to live across the street from us but he had moved. Most of the letter was about a tour we, the junior class, had taken of Alcatraz. That was all right. What got Mother was the last paragraph where I said that she had been coughing up blood and the doctors weren't sure what was wrong with her, but that we were hoping for the best.

This wasn't true. Mother took pride in her physical condition, considered herself a horse: "I'm a regular horse," she would reply when people asked about her health. For several years now I had been saying unpleasant things that weren't true and this habit of mine irked Mother greatly, enough to persuade her to send me to Dr. Murphy, in whose office I was sitting when she burned the letter. Dr. Murphy was our family physician and had no training in psychoanalysis but he took an interest in "things of the mind," as he put it. He had treated me for appendicitis and tonsilitis and Mother thought that he could put the truth into me as easily as he took things out of me, a hope Dr. Murphy did not share. He was basically interested in getting me to understand what I did, and lately he had been moving toward the conclusion that I understood what I did as well as I ever would.

Dr. Murphy listened to Mother's account of the letter, and what she had done with it. He was curious about the wording I had used and became irritated when Mother told him she had burned it. "The point is," she said, "he was supposed to be cured and he's not."

"Margaret, I never said he was cured."

"You certainly did. Why else would I have sent over a thousand dollars to the Thomasite mission?"

"I said that he was responsible. That means that James knows what he's doing, not that he's going to stop doing it."

"I'm sure you said he was cured."

"Never. To say that someone is cured you have to know what health is. With this kind of thing that's impossible. What do you mean by curing James, anyway?"

"You know."

"Tell me anyway."

"Getting him back to reality, what else?"

"Whose reality? Mine or yours?"

"Murphy, what are you talking about? James isn't crazy, he's a liar."

"Well, you have a point there."

"What am I going to do with him?"

"I don't think there's much you can do. Be patient."

"I've been patient."

"If I were you, Margaret, I wouldn't make too much of this. James doesn't steal, does he?"

"Of course not."

"Or beat people up or talk back."

"No."

"Then you have a lot to be thankful for."

"I don't think I can take any more of it. That business about leukemia last summer. And now this."

"Eventually he'll outgrow it, I think."

"Murphy, he's sixteen years old. What if he doesn't outgrow it? What if he just gets better at it?"

Finally Mother saw that she wasn't going to get any satisfaction from Dr. Murphy, who kept reminding her of her blessings. She said something cutting to him and he said something pompous back and she hung up. Dr. Murphy stared at the receiver. "Hello," he said, then replaced it on the cradle. He ran his hand over his head, a habit remaining from a time when he had hair. To show that he was a good sport he often joked about his baldness, but I had the feeling that he regretted it deeply. Looking at me across the desk, he must have wished that he hadn't taken me on. Treating a friend's child was like investing a friend's money.

"I don't have to tell you who that was."

I nodded.

Dr. Murphy pushed his chair back and swiveled it around so he could look out the window behind him, which took up most of the wall. There were still a few sailboats out on the Bay, but they were all making for shore. A woolly gray fog had covered the bridge and was moving in fast. The water seemed calm from this far up, but when I looked closely I could see white flecks everywhere, so it must have been pretty choppy.

"I'm surprised at you," he said. "Leaving something like that lying around for her to find. If you really have to do these things you could at least be kind and do them discreetly. It's not easy for your mother, what with your father dead and all the others somewhere else."

"I know. I didn't mean for her to find it."

"Well." He tapped his pencil against his teeth. He was not convinced professionally, but personally he may have been. "I think you ought to go home now and straighten things out."

"I guess I'd better."

"Tell your mother I might stop by, either tonight or tomorrow. And James—don't underestimate her."

While my father was alive we usually went to Yosemite for three or four days during the summer. My mother would drive and Father would point out places of interest, meadows where boom towns once stood, hanging trees, rivers that were said to flow upstream at certain times. Or he read to us; he had that grown-ups' idea that children love Dickens and Sir Walter Scott. The four of us sat in the back seat with our faces composed, attentive, while our hands and feet pushed, pinched, stomped, goosed, prodded, dug, and kicked.

One night a bear came into our camp just after dinner. Mother had made a tuna casserole and it must have smelled to him like something worth dying for. He came into the camp while we were sitting around the fire and stood swaying back and forth. My brother Michael saw him first and elbowed me, then my sisters saw him and screamed. Mother and Father had their backs to him but Mother must have guessed what it was because she immediately said, "Don't scream like that. You might frighten him and there's no telling what he'll do. We'll just sing and he'll go away."

We sang "Row Row Row Your Boat" but the bear stayed. He circled us several times, rearing up now and then on his hind legs to stick his nose into the air. By the light of the fire I could see his doglike face and watch the muscles roll under his loose skin like rocks in a sack. We sang harder as he circled us, coming closer and closer. "All right," Mother said, "enough's enough." She stood abruptly. The bear stopped moving and watched her. "Beat it," Mother said. The bear sat down and looked from side to side. "Beat it," she said again, and leaned over and picked up a rock.

"Margaret, don't," my father said.

She threw the rock hard and hit the bear in the stomach. Even in the dim light I could see the dust rising from his fur. He grunted and stood to his full height. "See that?" Mother shouted: "He's filthy. Filthy!" One of my sisters giggled. Mother picked up another rock. "Please, Margaret," my father said. Just then the bear turned and shambled away. Mother pitched the rock after him. For the rest of the night he loitered around the camp until he found the tree where we had hung our food. He ate it all. The next day we drove back to the city. We could have bought more supplies in the valley, but Father wanted to go and would not give in to any argument. On the way home he tried to jolly everyone up by making jokes, but Michael and my sisters ignored him and looked stonily out the windows.

Things were never easy between my mother and me, but I didn't underestimate her. She underestimate me. When I was little she suspected me of delicacy, because I didn't like being thrown into the air, and because when I saw her and the others working themselves up for a roughhouse I found somewhere else to be. When they did drag me in I got hurt, a knee in the lip, a bent finger, a bloody nose, and this too Mother seemed to hold against me, as if I arranged my hurts to get out of playing.

Even things I did well got on her nerves. We all loved puns except Mother, who didn't get them, and next to my father I was the best in the family. My speciality was the Swifty—"'You can bring the prisoner down,' said Tom condescendingly." Father encouraged me to perform at dinner, which must have been a trial for outsiders. Mother wasn't sure what was going on, but she didn't like it.

She suspected me in other ways. I couldn't go to the movies without her examining my pockets to make sure I had enough money to pay for the ticket. When I went away to camp she tore my pack apart in front of all the boys who were waiting in the bus outside the house. I would rather have gone without my sleeping bag and a few changes of underwear, which I had forgotten, than be made such a fool of. Her distrust was the thing that made me forgetful.

And she thought I was cold-hearted because of what happened the day my father died and later at his funeral. I didn't cry at my father's funeral, and showed signs of boredom during the eulogy, fiddling around with the hymnals. Mother put my hands into my lap and I left them there without moving them as though they were things I was holding for someone else. The effect was ironical and she resented it. We had a sort of reconciliation a few days later after I closed my eyes at school and refused to open them. When several teachers and then the principal failed to persuade me to look at them, or at some reward they claimed to be holding, I was handed over to the school nurse, who tried to pry the lids open and scratched one of them badly. My eye swelled up and I went rigid. The principal panicked and called Mother, who fetched me home. I wouldn't talk to her, or open my eyes, or bend, and they had to lay me on the back seat and when we reached the house Mother had to lift me up the steps one at a time. Then she put me on the couch and played the piano to me all afternoon. Finally I opened my eyes. We hugged each other and I wept. Mother did not really believe my tears, but she was willing to accept them because I had staged them for her benefit.

My lying separated us, too, and the fact that my promises not to lie any more seemed to mean nothing to me. Often my lies came back to her in embarrassing ways, people stopping her in the street and saying how sorry they were to hear that———. No one in the neighborhood enjoyed embarrassing Mother, and these situations stopped occurring once everybody got wise to me. There was no saving her from strangers, though. The summer after Father died I visited my uncle in Redding and when I got back I found to my surprise that Mother had come to meet my bus. I tried to slip away from the gentleman who had sat next to me but I couldn't shake him. When he saw Mother embrace me he came up and presented her with a card and told her to get in touch with him if things got any worse. She gave him his card back and told him to mind his own business. Later, on the way home, she made me repeat what I had said to the man. She shook her head. "It's not fair to people," she said, "telling them things like that. It confuses them." It seemed to me that Mother had confused the man, not I, but I didn't say so. I agreed with her that I shouldn't say such things and promised not to do it again, a promise I broke three hours later in conversation with a woman in the park.

It wasn't only the lies that disturbed Mother; it was their morbidity. This was the real issue between us, as it had been between her and my father. Mother did volunteer work at Children's Hospital and St. Anthony's Dining Hall, collected things for the St. Vincent de Paul Society. She was a lighter of candles. My brother and sisters took after her in this way. My father was a curser of the dark. And he loved to curse the dark. He was never more alive than when he was indignant about something. For this reason the most important act of the day for him was the reading of the evening paper.

Ours was a terrible paper, indifferent to the city that bought it, indifferent to medical discoveries—except for new kinds of gases that made your hands fall off when you sneezed—and indifferent to politics and art. Its business was outrage, horror, gruesome coincidence. When my father sat down in the living room with the paper Mother stayed in the kitchen and kept the children busy, all except me, because I was quiet and could be trusted to amuse myself. I amused myself by watching my father.

He sat with his knees spread, leaning forward, his eyes only inches from the print. As he read he nodded to himself. Sometimes he swore and threw the paper down and paced the room, then picked it up and began again. Over a period of time he developed the habit of reading aloud to me. He always started with the society section, which he called the parasite page. This column began to take on the character of a comic strip or a serial, with the same people showing up from one day to the next, blinking in chiffon, awkwardly holding their drinks for the sake of Peninsula orphans, grinning under sunglasses on the deck of a ski hut in the Sierras. The skiers really got his goat, probably because he couldn't understand them. The activity itself was inconceivable to him. When my sisters went to Lake Tahoe one winter weekend with some friends and came back excited about the beauty of the place, Father calmed them right down. "Snow," he said, "is overrated."

Then the news, or what passed in the paper for news: bodies unearthed in Scotland, former Nazis winning elections, rare animals slaughtered, misers expiring naked in freezing houses upon mattresses stuffed with thousands, millions; marrying priests, divorcing actresses, high-rolling oilmen building fantastic mausoleums in honor of a favorite horse, cannibalism. Through all this my father waded with a fixed and weary smile.

Mother encouraged him to take up causes, to join groups, but he would not. He was uncomfortable with people outside the family. He and my mother rarely went out, and rarely had people in, except on feast days and national holidays. Their guests were always the same, Dr. Murphy and his wife and several others whom they had known since childhood. Most of these people never saw each other outside our house and they didn't have much fun together. Father discharged his obligations as host by teasing everyone about stupid things they had said or done in the past and forcing them to laugh at themselves.

Though Father did not drink, he insisted on mixing cocktails for the guests. He would not serve straight drinks like rum-and-Coke or even Scotch-on-the-rocks, only drinks of his own devising. He gave them lawyerly names like "The Advocate," "The Hanging Judge," "The Ambulance Chaser," "The Mouthpiece," and described their concoction in detail. He told long, complicated stories in a near-whisper, making everyone lean in his direction, and repeated important lines; he also repeated the important lines in the stories my mother told, and corrected her when she got something wrong. When the guests came to the ends of their own stories he would point out the morals.

Dr. Murphy had several theories about Father, which he used to test on me in the course of our meetings. Dr. Murphy had by this time given up his glasses for contact lenses, and lost weight in the course of fasts which he undertook regularly. Even with his baldness he looked years younger than when he had come to the parties at our house. Certainly he did not look like my father's contemporary, which he was.

One of Dr. Murphy's theories was that Father had exhibited a classic trait of people who had been gifted children by taking an undemanding position in an uninteresting firm. "He was afraid of finding his limits," Dr. Murphy told me: "As long as he kept stamping papers and making out wills he could go on believing that he didn't *have* limits." Dr. Murphy's fascination with Father made me uneasy, and I felt traitorous listening to him. While he lived, my father would never have submitted himself for analysis; it seemed a betrayal to put him on the couch now that he was dead.

I did enjoy Dr. Murphy's recollections of Father as a child. He told me about something that happened when they were in the Boy Scouts. Their troop had been on a long hike and Father had fallen behind. Dr. Murphy and the others decided to ambush him as he came down the trail. They hid in the woods on each side and waited. But when Father walked into the trap none of them moved or made a sound and he strolled on without even knowing they were there. "He had the sweetest look on his face," Dr. Murphy said, "listening to the birds, smelling the flowers, just like Ferdinand the Bull." He also told me that my father's drinks tasted like medicine.

While I rode my bicycle home from Dr. Murphy's office Mother fretted. She felt terribly alone but she didn't call anyone because she also felt like a failure. My lying had that effect on her. She took it personally. At such times she did not think of my sisters, one happily married, the other doing brilliantly at Fordham. She did not think of my brother Michael, who had given up college to work with runaway children in Los Angeles. She thought of me. She thought that she had made a mess of her family.

Actually she managed the family well. While my father was dying upstairs she pulled us together. She made lists of chores and gave each of us a fair allowance. Bedtimes were adjusted and she stuck by them. She set regular hours for homework. Each child was made responsible for the next eldest, and I was given a dog. She told us frequently, predictably, that she loved us. At dinner we were each expected to contribute something, and after dinner she played the piano and tried to teach us to sing in harmony, which I could not do. Mother, who was an admirer of the Trapp family, considered this a character defect.

Our life together was more orderly, healthy, while Father was dying than it had been before. He had set us rules to follow, not much different really than the ones Mother gave us after he got sick, but he had administered them in a fickle way. Though we were supposed to get an allowance we always had to ask him for it and then he would give us too much because he enjoyed seeming magnanimous. Sometimes he punished us for no reason, because he was in a bad mood. He was apt to decide, as one of my sisters was going out to a dance, that she had better stay home and do something to improve herself. Or he would sweep us all up on a Wednesday night and take us ice-skating.

He changed after he learned about the cancer, and became more calm as the disease spread. He relaxed his teasing way with us, and from time to time it was possible to have a conversation with him which was not about the last thing that had made him angry. He stopped reading the paper and spent time at the window.

He and I became close. He taught me to play poker and sometimes helped me with my homework. But it wasn't his illness that drew us together. The reserve between us had begun to break down after the incident with the bear, during the drive home. Michael and my sisters were furious with him for making us leave early and wouldn't talk to him or look at him. He joked: though it had been a grisly experience we should grin and bear it—and so on. His joking seemed perverse to the others, but not to me. I had seen how terrified he was when the bear came into the camp. He had held himself so still that he had begun to tremble. When Mother started pitching rocks I thought he was going to bolt, really. I understood—I had been frightened too. The others took it as a lark after they got used to having the bear around, but for Father and me it got worse through the night. I was glad to be out of there, grateful to Father for getting me out. I saw that his jokes were how he held himself together. So I reached out to him with a joke: "'There's a bear outside,' said Tom intently." The others turned cold looks on me. They thought I was sucking up. But Father smiled.

When I thought of other boys being close to their fathers I thought of them hunting together, tossing a ball back and forth, making birdhouses in the basement, and having long talks about girls, war, careers. Maybe the reason it took us so long to get close was that I had this idea. It kept getting in the way of what we really had, which was a shared fear.

Toward the end Father slept most of the time and I watched him. From below, sometimes, faintly, I heard Mother playing the piano. Occasionally he nodded off in his chair while I was reading to him; his bathrobe would fall open then, and I would see the long new scar on his stomach, red as blood against his white skin. His ribs all showed and his legs were like cables.

I once read in a biography of a great man that he "died well." I assume the writer meant that he kept his pain to himself, did not set off false alarms, and did not too much inconvenience those who were to stay behind. My father died well. His irritability gave way to something else, something like serenity. In the last days he became tender. It was as though he had been rehearsing the scene, that the anger of his life had been a kind of stage fright. He managed his audience—us—with an old trouper's sense of when to clown and when to stand on his dignity. We were all moved, and admired his courage, as he intended we should. He died downstairs in a shaft of late afternoon sunlight on New Year's Day, while I was reading to him. I was alone in the house and didn't know what to do. His body did not frighten me but immediately and sharply I missed my father. It seemed wrong to leave him sitting up and I tried to carry him upstairs to the bedroom but it was too hard, alone. So I called up my friend Ralphy across the street. When he came over and saw what I wanted him for he started crying but I made him help me anyway. A couple of hours later Mother got home and when I told her that Father was dead she ran upstairs, calling his name. A few minutes later she came back down. "Thank God," she said, "at least he died in bed." This seemed important to her and I didn't tell her otherwise. But that night Ralphy's parents called. They were, they said, shocked at what I had done and so was Mother when she heard the story, shocked and furious. Why? Because I had not told her the truth? Or because she had learned the truth, and could not go on believing that Father had died in bed? I really don't know.

"Mother," I said, coming into the living room, "I'm sorry about the letter. I really am."

She was arranging wood in the fireplace and did not look at me or speak for a moment. Finally she finished and straightened up and brushed her hands. She stepped back and looked at the fire she had laid. "That's all right," she said. "Not bad for a consumptive."

"Mother, I'm sorry."

"Sorry? Sorry you wrote it or sorry I found it?"

"I wasn't going to mail it. It was a sort of joke."

"Ha ha." She took up the whisk broom and swept bits of bark into the fireplace, then closed the drapes and settled on the couch. "Sit down," she said. She crossed her legs. "Listen, do I give you advice all the time?"

"Yes."

"I do?"

I nodded.

"Well, that doesn't make any difference. I'm supposed to. I'm your mother. I'm going to give you some more advice, for your own good. You don't have to make all these things up, James. They'll happen anyway." She picked at the hem of her skirt. "Do you understand what I'm saying?"

"I think so."

"You're cheating yourself, that's what I'm trying to tell you.

When you get to be my age you won't know anything at all about life. All you'll know is what you've made up."

I thought about that. It seemed logical.

She went on. "I think maybe you need to get out of yourself more. Think more about other people."

The doorbell rang.

"Go see who it is," Mother said. "We'll talk about this later."

It was Dr. Murphy. He and mother made their apologies and she insisted that he stay for dinner. I went to the kitchen to fetch ice for their drinks, and when I returned they were talking about me. I sat on the sofa and listened. Dr. Murphy was telling Mother not to worry. "James is a good boy," he said. "I've been thinking about my oldest, Terry. He's not really dishonest, you know, but he's not really honest either. I can't seem to reach him. At least James isn't furtive."

"No," Mother said, "he's never been furtive."

Dr. Murphy clasped his hands between his knees and stared at them. "Well, that's Terry. Furtive."

Before we sat down to dinner Mother said grace; Dr. Murphy bowed his head and closed his eyes and crossed himself at the end, though he had lost his faith in college. When he told me that, during one of our meetings, in just those words, I had the picture of a raincoat hanging by itself outside a dining hall. He drank a good deal of wine and persistently turned the conversation to the subject of his relationship with Terry. He admitted that he had come to dislike the boy. Then he mentioned several patients of his by name, some of them known to Mother and me, and said that he disliked them too. He used the word "dislike" with relish, like someone on a diet permitting himself a single potato chip. "I don't know what I've done wrong," he said abruptly, and with reference to no particular thing. "Then again maybe I haven't done anything wrong. I don't know what to think any more. Nobody does."

"I know what to think," Mother said.

"So does the solipsist. How can you prove to a solipsist that he's not creating the rest of us?"

This was one of Dr. Murphy's favorite riddles, and almost any pretext was sufficient for him to trot it out. He was a child with a card trick.

"Send him to bed without dinner," Mother said. "Let him create that."

Dr. Murphy suddenly turned to me. "Why do you do it?" he asked. It was a pure question, it had no object beyond the satisfaction of his curiosity. Mother looked at me and there was the same curiosity in her face.

"I don't know," I said, and that was the truth.

Dr. Murphy nodded, not because he had anticipated my answer but because he accepted it. "Is it fun?"

"No, it's not fun. I can't explain."

"Why is it all so sad?" Mother asked. "Why all the diseases?"

"Maybe," Dr. Murphy said, "sad things are more interesting."

"Not to me," Mother said.

"Not to me, either," I said. "It just comes out that way."

After dinner Dr. Murphy asked Mother to play the piano. He particularly wanted to sing "Come Home Abbie, the Light's on the Stair."

"That old thing," Mother said. She stood and folded her napkin deliberately and we followed her into the living room. Dr. Murphy stood behind her as she warmed up. Then they sang "Come Home Abbie, the Light's on the Stair," and I watched him stare down at Mother intently, as if he were trying to remember something. Her own eyes were closed. After that they sang "O Magnum Mysterium." They sang it in parts and I regretted that I had no voice, it sounded so good.

"Come on, James," Dr. Murphy said as Mother played the last chords. "These old tunes not good enough for you?"

"He just can't sing," Mother said.

*   *   *

When Dr. Murphy left, Mother lit the fire and made more coffee. She slouched down in the big chair, sticking her legs straight out and moving her feet back and forth. "That was fun," she said.

"Did you and Father ever do things like that?"

"A few times, when we were first going out. I don't think he really enjoyed it. He was like you."

I wondered if Mother and Father had had a good marriage. He admired her and liked to look at her; every night at dinner he had us move the candlesticks slightly to right and left of center so he could see her down the length of the table. And every evening when she set the table she put them in the center again. She didn't seem to miss him very much. But I wouldn't really have known if she did, and anyway I didn't miss him all that much myself, not the way I had. Most of the time I thought about other things.

"James?"

I waited.

"I've been thinking that you might like to go down and stay with Michael for a couple of weeks or so."

"What about school?"

"I'll talk to Father McSorley. He won't mind. Maybe this problem will take care of itself if you start thinking about other people."

"I do."

"I mean helping them, like Michael does. You don't have to go if you don't want to."

"It's fine with me. Really. I'd like to see Michael."

"I'm not trying to get rid of you."

"I know."

Mother stretched, then tucked her feet under her. She sipped noisily at her coffee. "What did that word mean that Murphy used? You know the one?"

"Paranoid? That's where somebody thinks everyone is out to

get him. Like that woman who always grabs you after Mass—Frances."

"Not paranoid. Everyone knows what that means. Sol-something."

"Oh. Solipsist. A solipsist is someone who thinks he creates everything around him."

Mother nodded and blew on her coffee, then put it down without drinking from it. "I'd rather be paranoid. Do you really think Frances is?"

"Of course. No question about it."

"I mean really *sick?*"

"That's what paranoid *is*, is being sick. What do you think, Mother?"

"What are you so angry about?"

"I'm not angry." I lowered my voice. "I'm not angry. But you don't believe those stories of hers, do you?"

"Well, no, not exactly. I don't think she knows what she's saying, she just wants someone to listen. She probably lives all by herself in some little room. So she's paranoid. Think of that. And I had no idea. James, we should pray for her. Will you remember to do that?"

I nodded. I thought of Mother singing "O Magnum Mysterium," saying grace, praying with easy confidence, and it came to me that her imagination was superior to mine. She could imagine things as coming together, not falling apart. She looked at me and I shrank; I knew exactly what she was going to say. "Son," she said, "do you know how much I love you?"

The next afternoon I took the bus to Los Angeles. I looked forward to the trip, to the monotony of the road and the empty fields by the roadside. Mother walked with me down the long concourse. The station was crowded and oppressive. "Are you sure this is the right bus?" she asked at the loading platform.

"Yes."

"It looks so old."

"Mother—"

"All right." She pulled me against her and kissed me, then held me an extra second to show that her embrace was sincere, not just like everyone else's, never having realized that everyone else does the same thing. I boarded the bus and we waved at each other until it became embarrassing. Then Mother began checking through her handbag for something. When she had finished I stood and adjusted the luggage over my seat. I sat and we smiled at each other, waved when the driver gunned the engine, shrugged when he got up suddenly to count the passengers, waved again when he resumed his seat. As the bus pulled out my mother and I were looking at each other with plain relief.

I had boarded the wrong bus. This one was bound for Los Angeles but not by the express route. We stopped in San Mateo, Palo Alto, San Jose, Castroville. When we left Castroville it began to rain, hard; my window would not close all the way, and a thin stream of water ran down the wall onto my seat. To keep dry I had to stay away from the wall and lean forward. The rain fell harder. The engine of the bus sounded as though it were coming apart.

In Salinas the man sleeping beside me jumped up but before I had a chance to change seats his place was taken by an enormous woman in a print dress, carrying a shopping bag. She took possession of her seat and spilled over onto half of mine, backing me up to the wall. "That's a storm," she said loudly, then turned and looked at me. "Hungry?" Without waiting for an answer she dipped into her bag and pulled out a piece of chicken and thrust it at me. "Hey, by God," she hooted, "look at him go to town on that drumstick!" A few people turned and smiled. I smiled back around the bone and kept at it. I finished that piece and she handed me another, and then another. Then she started handing out chicken to the people in the seats near us.

Outside of San Luis Obispo the noise from the engine grew suddenly louder and just as suddenly there was no noise at all. The driver pulled off to the side of the road and got out, then got on again dripping wet. A few moments later he announced that the bus had broken down and they were sending another bus to pick us up. Someone asked how long that might take and the driver said he had no idea. "Keep your pants on!" shouted the woman next to me. "Anybody in a hurry to get to L.A. ought to have his head examined."

The wind was blowing hard around the bus, driving sheets of rain against the windows on both sides. The bus swayed gently. Outside the light was brown and thick. The woman next to me pumped all the people around us for their itineraries and said whether or not she had ever been where they were from or where they were going. "How about you?" She slapped my knee. "Parents own a chicken ranch? I hope so!" She laughed. I told her I was from San Francisco. "San Francisco, that's where my husband was stationed." She asked me what I did there and I told her I worked with refugees from Tibet.

"Is that right? What do you do with a bunch of Tibetans?"

"Seems like there's plenty of other places they could've gone," said a man in front of us. "Coming across the border like that. We don't go there."

"What do you do with a bunch of Tibetans?" the woman repeated.

"Try to find them jobs, locate housing, listen to their problems."

"You understand that kind of talk?"

"Yes."

"Speak it?"

"Pretty well. I was born and raised in Tibet. My parents were missionaries over there."

Everyone waited.

"They were killed when the Communists took over."

The big woman patted my arm.

"It's all right," I said.

"Why don't you say some of that Tibetan?"

"What would you like to hear?"

"Say 'The cow jumped over the moon.'" She watched me, smiling, and when I finished she looked at the others and shook her head. "That was pretty. Like music. Say some more."

"What?"

"Anything."

They bent toward me. The windows suddenly went blind with rain. The driver had fallen asleep and was snoring gently to the swaying of the bus. Outside the muddy light flickered to pale yellow, and far off there was thunder. The woman next to me leaned back and closed her eyes and then so did all the others as I sang to them in what was surely an ancient and holy tongue.

Acknowledgments

Grateful acknowledgment is made to the following publications in which these stories first appeared: *Antæus*: "An Episode in the Life of Professor Brooke," "In the Garden of the North American Martyrs," and "Next Door." *Atlantic Monthly*: "The Liar" and "Smokers." *Encounter*: "Wingfield." *Macmillan's Winter Tales* (anthology): "In the Garden of the North American Martyrs." *Mademoiselle*: "Face to Face." *TriQuarterly*: "Passengers" and "Hunters in the Snow." *Vogue*: "Maiden Voyage." *Willowsprings*: "Poaching."

Much of the time to write these stories has come to me in the form of grants from the National Endowment for the Arts, from the Creative Writing Center at Stanford University, and from the Mary Roberts Rinehart Foundation. My thanks. —T.W.

© by Elena Siebert

TOBIAS WOLFF was born in Birmingham, Alabama, and grew up in Washington State. He attended Oxford University and Stanford University, where he now teaches English and creative writing. He has received the Story Prize, both the Rea Award and PEN/Malamud Award for excellence in the short story, the *Los Angeles Times* Book Award, and the PEN/Faulkner Award.